OVERMAGE

THE SOUL BOUND SAGA
BOOK FIVE

JAMES E WISHER

SAND HILL PUBLISHING

Edited by: Janie Linn Dullard

Cover art by: B-Ro

ISBN: 978-1-68520-039-8

010120231.0

CHAPTER 1

Fane Morrow, better known to her followers as the archbishop, appeared in a roughhewn tunnel deep under the earth and immediately slammed her fist into the wall. Neither the dark-brown stone nor her pale, smooth skin cracked. Her immortal body could withstand far worse than that. Though she seriously doubted whether she could survive whatever spell the overmage inhabiting Samaritan's body used. It had torn her overseer apart with seeming ease.

She grimaced and turned away from the wall. Fane hadn't expected to be back here again so soon and she certainly hadn't expected to have to flee for her continued existence from the church's fortress. The artifact she assumed would lead her to this world's guardian dragon had instead contained the soul of an overmage, one of the former rulers of the Black Iron Empire and a powerful wizard.

Maybe more powerful than Fane herself. The idea that this world had even one wizard more powerful than her struck her as impossible. She had studied magic at the right hand of Amet Sur, the most powerful arcane lord of them all and a person she considered more god than man. Fane's immortal, undead body

1

made her nearly invincible. Only sunlight or mithril had a hope of killing her.

Now she could add whatever spell the bastard had used on her overseer to the list of things that might end her existence.

It was intolerable!

She'd gotten so close to achieving her goal only to have it stripped away at the last moment. One thing was certain. She would find a way to make the overmage—what did he say his name was—Khashair, yes, Fane would remember that name just long enough to engrave it on his tombstone.

"Hey."

She spun, ether crackling around her fingers, to find the youthful figure of Beastmaster walking toward her. The strongest of her many servants, Beastmaster looked like a twelve-year-old boy wearing a slightly too big brown robe. A three-eyed squirrel rode on his shoulder today. She'd seen him feed the disgusting thing a finger not that long ago.

Fane lowered her hands and relaxed. Despite his appearance, Beastmaster was several centuries old and a powerful wizard in his own right. If it came to a fight, she had no doubt which of them would fall, but given the strength of her new opponent, his help might be the difference between success and defeat.

"You seem a bit jumpy," Beastmaster said. "Did something happen at the fortress?"

"You could say that. I need to borrow your crystal ball. I'll tell you everything as we walk."

"Sure, no problem." He turned and went back the way he'd come. "Why did you come here instead of going to your citadel?"

Fane frowned. Why indeed? Some instinct had screamed at her not to go home, but rather come here instead. It made no sense. She was strongest at the citadel with its thick veil of corruption and many undead servants.

Maybe that was it. Khashair had a talent for destroying creatures made with corruption. Her servants wouldn't last long against the man.

"I'm not entirely certain myself." Fane told him what happened with Samaritan. "It looks like we have a new player in the game, a powerful one."

"Wow. Do you really think he's stronger than you?" He said it in an incredulous tone and Fane didn't blame him. Her mind used the same tone whenever she thought about what happened.

"I'm not sure if he's stronger than me in terms of raw power, but he clearly has a talent for destroying undead and creatures created with Black Bile and corruption. The effect we observed wasn't a ward, it was the overmage's spirit casting through the orb."

"I didn't even know something like that was possible."

Fane grit her teeth then forced herself to relax. "Neither did I. And it makes me wonder how much else Khashair knows that I don't. The prospect both excites and worries me in equal measure. Regardless of my feelings, the task of finding and controlling this world's hidden power remains unchanged."

She'd come far too close to admitting that what she sought was a guardian dragon. Though at this point it probably didn't matter if she told Beastmaster the whole truth or not.

Speaking of her host, he stopped in the middle of the tunnel and waved a hand at a blank section of wall. A door slid into the floor and beyond it waited a small chamber with a crystal ball resting on a round table.

"There you go. Anything else I can do?"

"Yes, join me in the link so you can see for yourself what we're dealing with. When we're finished, I'd like your opinion of Khashair. That's what the overmage calls himself."

Fane went inside and rested her fingers on the cool surface of the crystal ball. A moment later Beastmaster joined her and together they plunged their minds into the ether. Khashair had still worn Samaritan's mithril amulet, so she focused on that.

An instant later she found her psychic form floating over the fortress's training yard. Khashair, along with the forgeling, Gomo, and that obnoxious statue, stood in the center of the dirt yard. Fane hadn't the least idea what they were doing. Khashair looked up and down, left and right as if working a kink out of his neck.

A dark aura of corrupt ether swirled around him. How did he manage that with the amulet around his neck? The mithril should purify the ether as soon as it came into contact with any corruption.

"Why does the statue have a mithril amulet around its neck?" Beastmaster asked.

She'd been so focused on Khashair, Fane hadn't even noticed that he'd given the amulet to the golem. That, at least, made more sense. Such an item was too valuable to leave lying around while also being less than useful for someone that preferred to wield corrupt ether.

"Do you think Samaritan is still in there or did Khashair destroy his soul when he took over Samaritan's body?" Beastmaster asked.

Yet another question Fane had no answer for. "Why do you ask?"

"Well, assuming Samaritan's soul is still there, would that make them a soulbound pair? Who knows what kind of extra power that might provide."

She frowned as she considered the implication of Beastmaster's observation. Samaritan's soulmate had been killed, which meant Khashair's soul couldn't properly bond with his. But that didn't mean having two half souls in a single body wouldn't give him some sort of power boost. On this world, Fane, having been born on another world where soul bonds weren't a thing, was the only person she knew for sure had a complete soul. Granted it was a corrupted soul nearly replaced by pure ether, but still. She had long assumed that was one of the reasons she was so strong.

"I hadn't considered the possibility," Fane admitted. "If you're right, it would explain why he had the strength to overwhelm me, even if only for a moment."

She shifted her focus back to the courtyard. Khashair raised a hand and a circle of ether appeared. He'd opened a portal on his own, with no Black Bile to power the magic? Fane couldn't do that. In fact, she'd only ever seen arcane lords accomplish such a feat.

Had she underestimated his power that badly?

When all three had gone Beastmaster asked, "What now?"

What now indeed.

With an effort of will she returned their awarenesses to their bodies. As long as Khashair held on to the amulet, she could find them again wherever they went.

She stepped out into the tunnel and started pacing.

If—and it was a big if—Khashair had power even close to that of an arcane lord, then even Fane and Beastmaster combined had no hope of defeating him. She started to dismiss that idea out of hand then stopped herself. Underestimating this enemy wouldn't just result in a setback to the mission, it might well end with her destroyed.

"We need to know more about Khashair," she said at last. "Before his transformation, Samaritan mentioned a library in the Black Iron Empire. I've opened a portal there once, so returning should be no problem. I assume you have a supply of bile on hand. I can open a portal and send you through."

Beastmaster frowned. "Me? Aren't you going to do it yourself?"

"No. Someone has to remain behind and keep an eye on Khashair. Besides, if the library has windows, I'll only be able to work half the day. You can just power through nonstop."

Beastmaster shook his head. "I might not age anymore, but I still need to eat and sleep. Not as much as a regular human, but still. Can't you send one of the other overseers? You've got, what, two more at least? They actually don't need to sleep or eat."

"They also don't have the keenest wits. Anyway, I need them to keep the cult under control. You're the agent I have that's both smart enough and free at the moment. So you're going."

"Fine. I need to gather supplies. You know your way to the lab, right? I've got ten vials of Black Bile left." Beastmaster turned to leave, paused, and turned back. "Your human is still in one of my flesh pits. You'll need to feed and water him if you want to keep him alive."

Fane grimaced at Beastmaster's back as he went to get whatever he needed. She'd forgotten about the captive White Knight. Did she actually want to keep him alive? Samaritan might no longer exist for all she knew. No, she'd gone to all this trouble, tossing him a sack of jerky and a skin of water now and then shouldn't be too much trouble. She didn't have enough confidence to say for sure he would be of no further use and right now, Fane had no intention of throwing away anything that might give her an edge on Khashair, no matter how small.

Heaven knew she'd need every bit of help she could get to defeat that monster.

CHAPTER 2

J oran swallowed a groan when he woke. He didn't want
to open his eyes lest he find himself back in his own
room and last night only a dream. A deep breath flooded
his senses with the sweet scent of roses and he smiled.
Not a dream then.

He opened his eyes and stared up at the canopy that covered
Alexandra's bed. Bright sunlight streamed through the widow.
Beside him she shifted and he turned just enough to see the top
of her head sticking out from under the covers. No, definitely
not a dream.

While Alexandra might not have had any experience, she'd
more than made up for it with enthusiasm. None of the ladies of
the evening that Joran had visited over the years ever showed
even a fraction of her eagerness.

It had certainly been a night he'd never forget.

For more than one reason, alas. Before coming back to the
suite to celebrate his return from the Black Iron Empire with
Alexandra, they'd had dinner with the emperor and Marcus.
Joran told them everything he learned as well as what he feared
Samaritan had in mind for their nation. The looks of horror and

fear on the faces of the imperial family would stay with him for the rest of his life.

Did that fear play any part in Alexandra's later enthusiasm? He liked to think not, but after hearing something so horrifying, a life-affirming act might be just the thing to soothe your mind.

One way or the other, it was time to get up and going. The emperor had ordered him to find and secure the dragon's resting place as soon as possible. Joran's theory needed corroborating before they left. Even then, he wouldn't know for sure if he was right until they made the journey and confirmed the dragon's presence—quietly, lest they wake it themselves.

He pulled the cover aside and eased his legs off the side of the bed. Before he could even get his slippers on, a hand reached out and grabbed his arm. "You're leaving already?"

"Believe me, I'd very much prefer to stay here and snuggle with you for the rest of the year, but I doubt Samaritan will give us that much time. The sooner we find and secure the dragon's lair, the better. Once that's done, maybe I can actually take a proper rest."

She slid across the bed and pressed her chest to his back while her arms wrapped around him. "How much do you want to bet?"

He chuckled and squeezed her hand. "I don't want to bet. But I do want to finish the mission so I can get back in time for our wedding."

She kissed his shoulder. "You'd better. If you're not here, Father is liable to marry me off to someone else."

He turned and they shared a proper kiss. "I'm not leaving until tomorrow morning, so we have one more night together. The memories of which will motivate me to hurry back as soon as I can. But for now, I really do have to go."

Joran gently disengaged from Alexandra's far-too-welcoming arms and stood. He found his slippers and robe and shuffled out. Before the doors closed, he caught the faint rustle of the sheets being pulled back up over her head.

The sitting room was empty when he crossed it and entered the room he shared with Mia, his soulmate and adopted sister. She was already up, dressed, and pacing. A slight flush reddened her cheeks. No doubt sharing his mental reactions last night played a part in that.

"Morning," Joran said.

"I'm surprised you're up already. You didn't get much sleep last night." Her smile lit up the room. "That was amazing. Sharing with you was better than any sex I've ever had."

"It was everything you expected?"

"And then some. I'll have the servants get us some breakfast while you dress. I suppose we need to hit the books again today."

Joran smiled at Mia's disdain for anything scholarly. "Afraid so. Don't worry, I know exactly which book I need to check. Assuming I'm right, we can prepare for the journey north. It'll be you, me, and the dwarves to start. Once we confirm the dragon's location, the emperor plans to delegate security to the Fifth Legion."

"Are they back to full strength?" Mia asked.

"No, about two-thirds. That should be plenty to secure the entrance. Or so Alexandra said and I trust her judgement, especially about anything military."

Mia nodded and slipped out to see about breakfast, or maybe brunch given the hour.

Around noon, dressed and fed, Joran and Mia set out for the lab by way of the palace infirmary. He'd left Grub resting under the effect of a quick cure all and he wanted to see how his patient fared.

The infirmary door was marked with a red cross. Not wanting to disturb the patients, Joran opened it without knocking. Twenty beds ran the length of the room and happily today only four of them were occupied. Three women in white robes marked with a red cross like the one on the door tended the injured. One of them spotted Joran and hurried over. He put her age at around forty and when she smiled, warmth radiated from her. He'd met other healers like her, people called to care for others, some said by The One God, though he now knew that to be a lie. Perhaps some other power, like the angel Mia rescued, did the calling.

"Lord Den Cade, is all well?" she asked.

Joran smiled back. No way would he answer that question honestly. "As far as I know. I'm here to check on Grub. He should have woken from the healing trance by now."

"He did, several hours ago. After that he ate everything we put in front of him and went back to sleep. His friend hasn't left his side since you dropped him off."

Joran glanced down at the bed the furthest away on the right side to see Stoneheart seated in a too-tall chair beside it. Calling them friends would be a stretch, but since Grub lost his arm in the Black Iron Empire, Stoneheart had at least gotten to the point that he didn't expect an imminent betrayal from Grub.

"His arm?" Joran asked.

"Perfectly regrown. The power of a cure all never ceases to amaze me. If there's nothing you need, my lord, I should return to my post."

Joran nodded and led Mia down to the dwarves. As soon as he spotted them, Stoneheart leapt to his feet and touched fist to heart. "Lord Den Cade, how may I serve?"

"You can sit back down to start. I'm just here to see how Grub is healing. The nurse on duty seemed pleased."

Stoneheart looked down at Grub. "He's perfectly fine now, but seems determined to shirk his duties. Give the order and I'll wake him."

Joran chuckled. "No need for that yet. I've got some research to do, and preparations to make, then we'll be leaving to find the dragon's lair in the morning. So you know, you two have been assigned to my service until further notice. I trust you don't object."

"No, my lord. We'll be ready when you are."

Joran clapped Stoneheart on the shoulder. "Never doubted it."

Joran and Mia took their leave and when they were outside, she said, "Did you see how he looked at Grub? Protective instead of angry. I doubt we'll have much more in the way of arguments between those two."

"One can only hope. My guess is the bickering will resume, but it will be good-natured instead of mean-spirited. It'll be interesting to see which of us is right."

The walk to the lab took only minutes. Joran nodded to a few servants in passing. Happily, no nobles visited this part of the palace. A squad of Iron Guards controlled access to the lab and all of them saluted when Joran arrived.

"Any trouble, gentlemen?" he asked.

"No, Lord Den Cade," the unit commander said. "No one has been inside since you left for Dwarfhome, though Her Majesty did stalk by a few times and glare at us. We're all very pleased you made it back safe."

Joran grinned. "Me too. I've got some work to do so..."

"Right you are, my lord."

They opened the door for Joran and he slipped inside. Mia, to his surprise, joined him. The shelves held about half of the maximum number of reagents, but at least all the equipment was here and ready to use. He'd hoped to have the lab fully stocked by now, but their unexpected trip to the other side of the world had put that on the back burner.

In the center of the room, the main workbench held hundreds of volumes taken from the Forbidden Section of the imperial library. Joran hadn't even begun to read them all much less process the vast amount of knowledge. That might end up being his life's work, assuming he ever got a chance to start on it.

When the doors had closed, he said, "I figured you'd want to wait outside. Not afraid I'll put you to work reading?"

"You said you only had one book to check and I want to know where we're going so I can start planning the trip as soon as possible."

Joran shrugged his kit off his shoulder and pulled out the book he brought back from the castle library. He opened it, found the page that referenced the dragon waking, and set it on the workbench while he looked for the journal he'd read earlier.

"Where do you think it is?" Mia asked.

"The northern mountains." A bit of digging and he found the book he wanted. "This journal records the eruption of a volcano that was seen from hundreds of miles away. The northern mountains aren't volcanic, but a dragon exploding out of the ground might look like an eruption. Here it is."

Joran carried the journal over to the other book and compared the dates. They were identical. That couldn't be a coincidence.

"Getting there's going to be tricky." Mia stood, reading over his shoulder. "That's actually west of the empire, well into the Land of the Blood Drinkers. No chance we'll be able to take a dragon ship all the way. I'm not even sure how we'll get the legion there without fighting another war."

"There's a map on the shelf over there. Let's see if we can figure it out."

Mia grabbed the rolled-up map and they spread it out on top of a bunch of books. She stabbed a spot about a hundred miles west of the border and north into the jagged peaks of The Broken Fang Mountains. "That's our target location."

Just getting their small team to the site was going to be a nightmare. He had no idea how the Fifth would manage it.

At last Joran shook his head. "Let's just find out if the dragon is actually there. If it found a new place to nap, we might be worrying for nothing."

"Maybe." Mia didn't look away from the map and a little frown creased her lips. "But when's the last time anything went our way?"

Both of them knew the answer to that question and the less said about it, the better.

CHAPTER 3

Khashair stepped through the portal and emerged in the center of a ruined collection of stone buildings. Of course, if you'd never been to this outpost before, you might think they were just piles of broken rock. Only a single, mostly intact tower still stood, though it had lost its roof and top floor. To think the dragon came this far and did this much damage. Truly a vindictive creature.

Beside him the forgeling, Gomo, looked around at the ruin with a frown creasing his quill-covered face. The red-skinned demon dwarf had chosen to remain with Khashair rather than flee with the female vampire. He hadn't bothered to ask why and as long as Gomo did nothing to hinder his conquest of this primitive continent, he wouldn't send the demon back to Hell the hard way.

This is my hideout. Why did you bring us here?

Samaritan's voice echoed in his mind. Khashair didn't obliterate him simply because having a second half soul gave him extra power. And he'd need it given his lack of allies.

"This was my hideout before it was yours. I built this little complex should the worst happen and I needed to flee the empire. The servants I left were certainly slain when the dragon came, but the supplies should be fine."

"Who are you talking to?" Gomo asked.

Khashair tapped the side of his head. "Samaritan is still rattling around in here. I simply don't care to spend the mental energy to speak with him telepathically. Now, let's see if my supplies survived as well as I hope they did. Automaton, activate search and recovery protocol."

The black iron statue gave a shudder, turned toward the tower, and marched forward. Now that Khashair had returned to life, the automaton had returned to its proper and more limited function as a citadel guardian control unit. Despite the name, the unit didn't have to be stationed in a citadel to handle its duties. Khashair had designed this one to serve as a sort of subcommander for his combat troops. Though far from a tactical genius, it had vastly more intellect than the regular black iron golems.

He and Gomo followed along behind the stomping automaton. At the base of the tower it ripped a barely attached door off its hinges and tossed it aside. That seemed unnecessarily destructive. Khashair made a mental note to check the unit's logic spells before he gave it any important tasks.

On the bottom floor of the tower, the golem strode over to the far-right corner and pointed. Khashair grinned when a section of floor vanished, revealing a trapdoor. If that spell still functioned after all this time, surely the better protected items below survived.

I had no idea that was there.

"Why would you? You're neither a citadel defense automaton nor much of a wizard. Besides, I doubt you even looked for a hidden door, did you?"

Gomo flicked a glance his way, but didn't comment.

No, I suppose I didn't. I spent most of my time on the upper floors.

There was a book on the basics of magic that advanced my understanding a great deal.

Khashair felt no need to comment as he followed the automaton down a flight of stone stairs. The familiar scent of Black Bile stung his nostrils as power swirled around him. Such useful stuff. Enough Black Bile, combined with the will to use it, would allow a wizard to change the world or a dragon to destroy it.

He shuddered at the memory of his last moment in his old body. The dragon's black flames had washed over him like a tidal wave. After a moment of exquisite pain, his soul had fled to the orb he prepared. One of his apprentices should have come to free him within days, but the dragon had proven more destructive than even his worst fears. At least the backup plan had worked, albeit after far too long a wait.

At the bottom of the stairs they entered a long hall with niches carved into it. Each niche held a single black iron golem —fifty in total. Not the largest force in the world, but a nearly indestructible one. Streams of magic shot out from his raised hands and penetrated the golems' heads. Their eyes all flashed once, acknowledging the activation command.

"That's a start. Let's check out the storeroom."

He strode down the hall to a closed metal door. This also opened at a touch of magic.

Why do you think of it as magic and not ether?

"Because it doesn't matter what you call it. Magic, ether, chaos, divine energy, it's all just different names for the same thing. Since it powers our spells, we call it magic. Now be silent lest I decide keeping you around isn't worth the power boost."

Samaritan obliged him, but Khashair understood the man held no fear of death. Nothing he threatened Samaritan with could be worse than what had already been done to him. He hated dealing with people, or in this case barely embodied souls, that had no fear. Manipulating fear was a wonderful way to get what you wanted. All the overmages excelled at it.

Putting his psychic companion out of his mind, so to speak, Khashair focused on the large, square room in front of him. Everything looked exactly as he'd left it, which came as a surprise given the damage aboveground. Black iron swords by the score stood upright in racks, hundreds of potions gleamed on shelves, and thick leather breastplates studded with black iron sat on forms along the back wall.

A fair arsenal by any measure. Now he just needed to find soldiers to wield it. Loyal soldiers, ideally.

You can use the cultists. They're just waiting for the word to strike. This gear plus your golems would make them unstoppable.

Khashair considered, not even annoyed that Samaritan spoke despite his warning. The cultists of The One True God were fanatics and if he could convince them that he was the actual archbishop rather than that vampire, they would probably follow him eagerly.

Only the overseers know what she looks like. The regular cultists only know the name.

"Finding them will be the hard part. If they work in cells, only their masters will know where they all are. I can't imagine they keep a list. Well, torturing the information out of a minor demonic spirit shouldn't be too difficult."

"Is there anything you want me to do?" Gomo asked.

Khashair glanced at the forgeling. "Not at the moment, but when the battle begins, your magic will be useful. Until then, you will stay at my side."

"You don't trust me?" The demon's smile revealed his fangs.

"No, but if you give me a reason, I'll be happy to bind you properly. Rest assured, when I'm finished, you won't be able to take a breath without my permission. The only reason I haven't is that I find bound demons too rigid in their obedience. Don't make me regret my generosity."

"I won't, but I am getting sick of being passed around between you mortal wizards like a piece of livestock."

Khashair strode over to the rack holding his potions, set his orb on the top, and pulled out a vial filled with bubbling black liquid. Liquid Death, the purest form of Black Bile. A single drop could kill an entire city.

He spun and hurled the vial at Gomo.

It shattered, sending the thick goo running down his chest to be quickly absorbed.

Gomo's bloodred eyes flashed and he clutched his chest. "What did you do to me?"

"I made sure you wouldn't have to worry about being passed around like livestock. Should anyone succeed in taking control of you, the Liquid Death will annihilate your essence, thus freeing you from ever worrying about anything again. Now, let's see about finding those cultists. Automaton, secure the amulet and organize my defenses."

The golem's eyes flashed and Khashair transferred control of the new units. Should anyone be stupid enough to come here looking to cause trouble, they'd quickly wish they hadn't.

CHAPTER 4

Beastmaster emerged from the portal Fane opened and looked around at an empty clearing surrounded by weird black trees. No library or buildings of any sort. Just black dirt under a leaden sky. No animals called out and the air stank with the faint scent of rot. This was easily the worst place Beastmaster had ever visited and he lived underground.

He spun around, mouth open to complain, only to find the portal closed. His pet three-eyed squirrel darted out of his pocket and climbed up on his shoulder.

She looked around and squeaked.

"You're right, we should teleport back and tell Fane that she dropped us in the wrong place, but she was in an awfully bad mood before we left. Making her even grumpier wouldn't be a good idea. Let's have a look around. Maybe the library isn't that far away."

His pet squeaked again and blinked all three of her eyes at him.

Beastmaster patted her head a couple times before closing his eyes and sending his sight soaring upward. The ether was really corrupted, but for an immortal wizard used to dealing with Black Bile, that was only a minor annoyance.

From a thousand feet up, he saw nothing that looked like civilization, only more dirt and black trees. A few hundred yards from his current position, he spotted another clearing, this one with a hole in the ground.

That was strange enough to warrant a quick look. Maybe this land had giant gophers. He'd never experimented with a giant gopher. The trick would be getting it back to his lab. Teleporting with his squirrel was simple, but anything much bigger would be an issue.

His sight zipped down and through the opening. Beyond it he found stone tunnels, manmade ones. No gophers then. Pity.

On the plus side, maybe this was the library he was supposed to visit. The clearing was only a hundred or so yards away from where he arrived. That wasn't so bad.

Pulling his sight back he focused on the location and became one with the ether. An instant later he stood looking at the hole. He sensed no wards or defenses beyond a simple teleportation barrier that didn't even extend into the clearing. With a shrug he hopped down into the tunnel. The place reminded him a little of home, though the stink of Black Bile was stronger here than in his lair.

Beastmaster strolled along the passage, senses magical and mundane alert for any danger. A couple minutes brought him to an intersection. Hmm, left or right? Strange symbols consisting of straight vertical and horizontal lines marked each branch, but they meant nothing to him. He activated a translation spell, but the symbols fought the magic, refusing to divulge their meaning.

Interesting. The symbols themselves had to be magical since there were no wards on the complex.

Beastmaster shrugged and turned his head a fraction to look at his pet. "What do you think?"

She sniffed, squeaked, and pointed her nose right.

"Works for me." He turned right and resumed his leisurely pace.

Fane would no doubt laugh at him for paying attention to a squirrel, but he'd made her senses as sharp as possible and she even had a boost to her intelligence. She wasn't actually smart, but when it came to tracking, she was better than most humans. Beastmaster made his pets to serve particular purposes and this was hers. Ignoring her would just be stupid.

At the end of the passage, he found a closed door with a headless black statue beside it. It looked like the one Khashair had with him at the fortress. "So were you supposed to protect this room? And who cut your head off?"

The statue ignored him which didn't surprise Beastmaster in the least. He pushed the door open and glanced around the room. Not that there was much to see. Just to be sure, he walked over to the pit in the center and looked down. A shallow pool of Black Bile, maybe an inch deep, filled the bottom. More of the strange symbols he'd seen earlier surrounded the pit. A magic circle but for what purpose he had no clue.

Beastmaster shook his head. No books here. Whatever the room's function, he neither knew nor cared. Time to check the other branch.

He retraced his steps and tried the left-hand branch of the tunnel. This one held numerous closed doors all labeled with the familiar symbols. Figuring out what those meant would be a great help he felt certain. If he expended enough power, he might force a translation, but if he was wrong, he might end up erasing the symbols instead.

Better not to risk it yet, not when he might find a translation key somewhere.

The first four rooms held complete, if dusty, workshops. They were well stocked for both alchemy and artifact creation. Better stocked than Beastmaster's own workshop. The next two rooms held replacement supplies, then came another four workshops. This complex appeared to be designed for producing magical items in large quantities. He'd never seen or heard of anything like it.

Unfortunately, it was becoming painfully clear that this wasn't a library. No doubt Fane had simply assumed this was the place Samaritan mentioned. That would be just like her. And now he had to work out a solution other than giving up and going home.

"One door left. Think we'll find anything useful?"

A shiver ran through her feet into his shoulder and she scrambled down into his pocket. Was that a good sign or a bad sign for what waited behind the final door? He didn't know but he'd wasted as much time here as he cared to.

The final door opened as easily as the others and inside he found a bile pit, a far smaller one than what he was familiar with, along with black iron tongs and a crucible for collecting samples. Of greater interest was the small collection of books neatly arranged on a two-level bookcase as far from the pit as the room allowed.

"Not exactly a library," Beastmaster muttered as he strode over to the shelf.

He offered a silent word of thanks when he opened the first book and found it written in Imperial. Finally, something he could read. He skimmed the pages. It appeared to be a record of the magical experiments that took place in this facility. The descriptions were tantalizingly brief and had nothing to do with his mission.

The next five books were like the first and he suspected detailed every ritual and item created here since the complex was built. Incredibly interesting and totally useless. Hopefully the last book would yield something more valuable.

He opened it up and grinned. An atlas detailing the complex network of pipes that carried Black Bile to every corner of the empire as well as every pit that allowed access. The nearest pit was in the basement of a citadel that belonged to an overmage named Krixious. He kept reading until he found what he needed: the location of Khashair's citadel. It waited about five hundred miles southwest. A fair distance if you had to walk.

Lucky for Beastmaster, he knew how to fly.

He pocketed the book and retreated to the exit where he carved and empowered a marking rune just outside the wards. Now he could return whenever he wanted. Here he could conduct his own experiments and Fane would know nothing about them.

And while Beastmaster didn't really want to rebel against Fane, he wouldn't mind getting strong enough to make her stop bullying him. Not to mention the idea of having a secret place of his own made him smile and that was reason enough to claim the lab.

He flew out of the clearing, orientated himself southwest, and shot off in pursuit of his goal. Hopefully he'd find Khashair's journal waiting on a bedside stand for him. He had no desire to have to visit every place listed in the book looking for clues. At least not right now.

When the current crisis had been sorted out would be soon enough to begin his little side project.

CHAPTER 5

Gaius's toe started tapping again and he forced it to stop. A true White Knight had more discipline than that. He, along with a force of brother White Knights and imperial alchemists several hundred strong were jammed into the hold of an imperial dragon ship on their way east to reclaim a church fortress from the insane wizard that had taken it over. Given that the ship was intended to carry a force of one hundred soldiers, more than doubling that made for a cramped journey. They had to sleep in shifts or on the floor given the lack of cots, and the less said about the head, the better.

Not that anyone complained. A White Knight would sooner cut out his own tongue than show that kind of weakness. An announcement had gone out from the bridge that they'd arrive at the fortress in a few hours. When they did, Gaius intended to avenge his fallen brothers.

A task easier said than done given the power of the creature the wizard controlled. That bizarre spider thing had slaughtered his brothers like they were children rather than the finest warriors in the empire. Only luck and careful planning allowed

Gaius to escape when the fortress fell. Now they would need even more luck. Or at least more alchemist's fire.

"Thirty minutes to drop." The announcement came over one of the pipes built into the wall to carry the captain's voice to all corners of the ship.

Finally. The knights all stopped whatever they were doing, lined up, and followed Knight Commander Valen to the drop area. Heavy ropes with a loop in the bottom to put your foot would allow them to quickly reach the ground.

Gaius shivered and moved into place. He'd been granted the honor of descending with the first unit. He put his foot as far as it would go into the loop and took a tight hold of the rope. He'd learned many things in his training, but they never covered this. He overheard one of the combat alchemists telling the commander that the trick was to hold on tight and not look down.

That seemed like good advice and Gaius intended to follow it to the letter.

Gaius had just pulled his gauntlets back on after drying his hands for the fifth time when the captain said, "One minute!"

He had time for one last check of the loop and to get a tight grip before a four-foot-square trapdoor opened in the floor. A sudden, unswallowable lump formed in Gaius's throat. That looked way too much like the trapdoor on a gallows for comfort.

Eyes clamped shut, he started to descend.

Seconds later his feet hit the ground. Gaius's eyes snapped open and he found himself in the fortress courtyard. He hurried to get free of the rope. As soon as he did, it retracted into the ship to let the next group descend.

"Defensive positions!" Valen said.

The order immediately snapped Gaius out of his momentary shock. He drew his sword and shrugged the shield off his back before moving to stand beside the nearest knight, a man ten years his senior with a long scar on his cheek. They faced the smashed keep door, faces grim. Every moment Gaius expected the spider monster to come boiling out to slaughter them all.

Nothing happened and ten minutes later the entire force of knights and alchemists were standing in the courtyard ready for battle.

"First unit, slow advance on me. Second unit, secure the main gate. The rest of you are on reserve alert. The halls are too narrow for a large group to fight. If we fall, Unit Three will take our place and so on until we control the keep. Understood?"

"Yes, sir!" the White Knights all shouted in unison.

"Then in The One God's name, advance!"

Unit One marched forward in lockstep.

Each breath Gaius drew he feared might be his last. The monster had to be here somewhere, just waiting for them to lower their guard so it could strike.

He forced the thought away. If it wanted to kill them all, it had no need to wait. Twenty of them would be no more of a threat than if Gaius had come alone.

He stomped through the rotten ruins of the door and tried not to think about Commander Florens. His soul was no doubt with The One God now. That knowledge should have comforted him, but Gaius found it bitter. He wanted his brothers alive and at his side, not enjoying whatever reward they'd earned.

An unworthy thought, but an honest one. He would have to find a priest next God's Day so he could confess. Assuming he was still alive.

The team cleared hall after hall and room after room. The damage was astonishing, but of the monster they saw no sign. Nor did they find any sign of their brothers or the wizard. The keep felt empty, abandoned. A ghost seemed more likely to show up than a living man.

Best not to dwell on that either.

At last, they stopped in front of the door to the basement where the artifact was supposed to be kept. It had been broken down.

"I fear we may be too late," Gaius said without thinking.

Valen shot him a look, but there was no heat in it. He knew as well as anyone what Gaius had seen here. "You might be right, but we have to confirm that the artifact has been taken. If you wish to wait here..."

"No, thank you, sir. I need to see."

Valen nodded. "Then let's go. Single file. Everyone stay alert."

That last order was hardly necessary. Gaius doubted anyone would be relaxing in the near future.

At the bottom of the steps Gaius froze, keeping the others from advancing. The bodies of his brothers lay in pools of dried blood. Some of them had been torn apart. Others had their heads caved in. He'd never seen anything like the horror spread out before him.

A gentle hand moved him to one side so the others could get off the steps. Gaius didn't even notice who had touched him. He couldn't look away from the death and destruction. His worst nightmares didn't begin to compare.

"The artifact is gone, sir," one of the knights said, snapping him out of his dark thoughts.

And now that he could actually think about something other than the dead knights surrounding him Gaius realized something. "The spider monster didn't kill them."

Valen turned away from the knight that reported the missing artifact to look at him. "How do you know?"

"Whenever it killed someone, it absorbed the body and grew larger. If it had killed everyone, their bodies would be gone. I don't know what did this, but it had to be something else."

Valen scowled and rubbed the bridge of his nose. "Assuming you're right, and I see no reason to doubt your assessment, the next question is, does that fact matter? The artifact is gone and there's no one left to rescue. We can give our brothers a proper burial while we wait for orders. What happens next is well above my rank."

"I don't know, sir, but these men weren't killed with magic. If the spider monster didn't kill them and the wizard didn't do it, then who did? It certainly raises the prospect of a third party, don't you think?"

"If you're trying to make an already horrible day worse, Gaius, you're doing a fine job." Valen raised a hand to stop him when he tried to apologize. "No, you're also right. I'll include your assessment when I write my report. But right or wrong, it's still out of my control. His Holiness and the emperor will decide what happens next."

Gaius made the circle over his heart. "May The One God give them the wisdom to make the correct decision."

All the men around him made the circle as well and as one said, "So say we all."

CHAPTER 6

Joran and Alexandra sat side by side on the sofa in her suite and studied the map spread out on the table in front of them. She inched closer and pressed her shoulder to his. Joran smiled and leaned back. Having to leave her, especially after the last two days, was the hardest part of the trip. Well, the beginning part of the trip at least. No doubt the many monsters and enemies they'd have to deal with in the mountains would help take his mind off of missing her.

"So what do you think?" he asked. "I know we've been over it a few times, but this is the last chance to make changes before we leave."

She shook her head. "It's the best possible route given your destination. I see no issues before you leave the dragon ship at our northwestern-most border fort. After you cross the border, you enter the unknown. No scout or merchant has ever entered the Land of the Blood Drinkers. What little we know comes from ancient texts. The entire nation is basically a huge empty spot on the map. It's one of the reasons we haven't invaded yet."

"None of that is terribly encouraging. I'm glad we only need to go a hundred or so miles in."

"I didn't want to be encouraging. I want to scare you, so you don't underestimate the risks you'll face."

"Mission accomplished then. I certainly have no intention of underestimating the dangers. Though given everything that's happened over the last few months, my sense of danger may be warped. We are marching to the home of the most dangerous creature on the planet, however, so it's kind of hard to underestimate that. Any final words of advice?"

"Don't fight unless you have to. Get in and out as fast as you can. Come back to me in one piece."

"Good advice." He leaned in and kissed her. "We should be back in a month at most, hopefully with good news. Though at this point, I'm not exactly certain what would constitute good news: finding the dragon at home or it having moved."

"I'm not sure either, but whichever it is, we'll deal with it when you return. Good luck."

He stood and collected his map. "Thanks."

Joran walked over to his room and opened the door. Mia had her gear packed and ready, the mithril sword hanging at her side. She wore no armor, but they'd packed some on the dragon ship already.

Joran slung his fully loaded kit over his shoulder. "Ready?"

"As I'll ever be. Stoneheart and Grub should be at the landing field waiting for us." She joined him at the door and whispered, "That was a very nice kiss you two had."

Joran shook his head at his soulmate's one-track mind. "I'm glad you enjoyed it too."

With a final wave, Joran led the way down the hall to their usual side entrance, drawing salutes from the palace guards on duty. He nodded in passing but didn't slow his stride. The sooner they took off, the sooner they'd get back.

Five minutes brought them to their dragon ship, one of two remaining in the landing field. Once they left, only the emperor's personal ship would remain. The dwarves were still working to repair the one that got shot down by rebel geomancers and the White Knights hadn't returned from reclaiming their fortress. Joran expected a report from the east soon, not that it was his problem to worry about.

Stoneheart and Grub stood at the foot of the boarding ramp. Stoneheart offered a crisp salute when they arrived, but Grub just nodded.

"How's the arm?" Joran asked.

"Good as new, thanks. My first and hopefully last encounter with a cure all was quite an experience. I'm uncertain how best to describe the feeling of your arm growing back beyond 'not nearly as painful as I expected.'"

Joran grinned, pleased to see Grub fully recovered. He intended to use the flight to learn everything he could about magic. Considering where they were going, they'd need every possible advantage.

"Did Her Majesty have any more thoughts on the trip?" Stoneheart asked.

"Not beyond warning me once again to be careful. I told her I'd do my best given our mission. Let's go, daylight's burning."

Joran led the way up the ramp. Hard to believe that flying on a dragon ship had been one of his biggest fears once. Now that he knew what was out in the world, he found flying hardly made it onto his list.

————

Alexandra stared at the closed door of her suite, her face twisted in a frown of disappointment. He was gone again. Joran had barely made it back from the Black Iron Empire. By The One God, how insane did that sound? And now he was leaving again on a potentially even more dangerous mission. Part of her, a big part, wanted to argue that he'd done enough. That he could leave finding the dragon to someone else.

But even as she thought it, she knew Joran and Mia were the ones best suited to handle the job. The Iron Princess in her said suck it up and have a little faith. The part of her that finally realized she loved Joran said to hell with that, keep him close and safe. Both halves of her were right, but as always, the Iron Princess ended up winning.

She brushed a hair out of her face. Maybe she should take time to get her hair cut. It had grown out since getting back from Stello Province. At this point anything that distracted her from Joran's danger would be welcome.

A knock on the door brought her up short. There was no way Joran had come back again. One goodbye had been bad enough.

Two long strides brought her to the door and she pulled it open. One of the palace messengers, a boy around twelve in a crimson and gold tunic held out a sealed scroll about three inches long. "A message just arrived for you, Majesty."

She took it, happy to have the distraction she'd been looking for. "Thank you."

He bowed and hurried back up the hall.

Alexandra returned to the couch, broke the sword-and-shield symbol that marked it as having come from the army, and started reading.

Line by line the news only got worse. The advance team found the church fortress empty save for bodies, and the artifact gone. Gaius, the sole survivor of the initial attack, argued strongly that some new party had arrived and killed the remaining knights. Beyond that, no details were offered. The message ended with a request for orders.

Alexandra tapped her chin. Sending the Fourth Legion now would be a waste of time since they'd find no enemy to fight. As for the alchemists, she'd like to get them back to Tiber as soon as possible. That would restore the First and Second to full strength.

But she couldn't make the decision on her own. She needed to speak to Father first. Lucky for her it wasn't a court day which meant he should be in his private office or his suite.

No sense in delaying the inevitable.

She got up and strode out the door and up the hall. It wasn't that far to Father's quarters. She passed servants and guards, all of whom bowed, curtsied, or saluted as was appropriate. And she ignored them like a proper imperial noble. She just couldn't get used to the way Joran acted so familiarly with the servants. Not that she thought his actions were disingenuous, they just felt wrong for a nobleman. Sweet, but wrong.

She tried Father's suite first and happily found a full dozen imperial guards on duty. There would only be that many if he were still here, which saved her from having to check his office.

They all saluted and the unit commander asked, "How may we help you, Princess?"

"I need to speak with Father. A message of some importance has arrived."

"Of course." The unit commander thumped the door and opened it a crack. "Princess Alexandra is here, Your Imperial Majesty."

"Send her in," Father said in a muffled voice.

He opened the door the rest of the way and Alexandra strode through. She found her father in his favorite leather chair, a book resting in his lap. How long since she'd seen him take even an hour to rest? Barring when he was sick, she couldn't actually remember.

Father met her gaze and smiled, wearily she thought. "Joran's on his way, right?"

"Yes, Father. But another matter has come to my attention. The advance team has reached the church fortress." Alexandra gave him a summary of the report. When she offered him the scroll he shook his head. "I thought to have the alchemists return here and the Fourth stand down."

"Has Septimus been told?"

"Not by me. I assume the knight commander would have sent his own message. Does it matter? If there's no enemy, there's nothing for our people to do. The White Knights can repair and occupy the fortress without our help."

"True, but why don't you wait on the recall until I hear from the pope. The Fourth can stand down at once."

"Understood, Father. Why..?" She clamped her jaw shut. It wasn't worth the argument to finish her question.

"If you have something to say, say it."

"Why are you being deferential to the pope now? The weasel has fed us nothing but half-truths and outright lies."

"I can't argue with you there, but Septimus knows more about what's going on than we do. I don't want to antagonize him until we know everything he does. Of course, I might be wrong and he's as in the dark as we are, but if that's the case, then we'll really need to work together to figure out what's going on."

Though she didn't like it, Alexandra found no fault in her father's logic. "In that case, I'll contact the Fourth and wait for your word on the rest."

"Good girl. I'll be honest, the artifact, whatever it was, worries me a good deal more than a few dead knights. Any time we've had anything to do with magic, a lot of our people ended up dying."

Alexandra knew that firsthand. She hoped this time would be different, but deep down, all her instincts screamed that something horrible was coming.

CHAPTER 7

Khashair left his defense automaton to protect the supply depot and strode out of the basement storage room with Gomo on his heels. The time had come to start building his army. According to Samaritan's memories, the creatures called overseers ran small groups of cultists throughout the Tiberian Empire. He hoped to collect at least a few hundred soldiers. Once equipped with black iron weapons and armor, they'd be a match for ten times that many opponents. They still wouldn't be enough to control the entire territory, but it would be a start.

Samaritan seemed to think finding the overseers would be a problem, but he was wrong. They were made using Black Bile and Khashair knew more about using that power source than anyone else. Finding their unique magical signatures would take time, but he'd do it.

Before he had a chance to reach for the ether Gomo asked, "Anything you want me to do?"

"For now, be silent. If something else comes to mind, I'll let you know."

Putting the demon dwarf out of his mind, Khashair reached

for the pool of Black Bile under the tower. Its power rushed into him and he sent his awareness flying out. He blurred his vision, ignoring everything save the ether, or more specifically the many threads of corruption running through it. With so much Black Bile under the empire, he had no trouble gathering all the power he needed to accelerate his search.

Sometime later he found the first blip of demonic essence. Honing in on it, he sharpened his vision and found himself in a forest overgrown with parasitic vines. His search quickly brought him to a cave at the edge of the forest where a human body with melted skin wearing a hooded cloak sat silently on a boulder. The demon spirit that animated it looked barely stronger than an imp. Hardly a threat to him.

Khashair looked around again. He was still in the middle of nowhere. Why in the world did the vampire order her minion to stay in such an out-of-the-way location?

He shrugged, pulled back a quarter mile or so, and marked a spot in the ether. A blink of his eyes returned his spirit to his new body.

"Find one?" Gomo asked. "You've been standing there for so long I'd begun to wonder if something went wrong."

Khashair shrugged. "These things take as long as they take. I'm going to question the first overseer. You will watch my back while I work."

He pointed and a portal opened. Two long strides later and Khashair stood in the clearing he marked earlier. Gomo stepped out beside him a moment later and the portal closed.

When they reached the cave, the overseer had moved to the entrance to face them. With the sun revealing more details, the thing's melted flesh looked even more disgusting. Khashair shook his head. This was what you got when amateurs played with Black Bile. He would have pitied the thing had he been capable of such a weak emotion.

"The archbishop warned me you might show up." Even the

overseer's voice was wrong. It sounded thick and phlegmy, like some of the bile got stuck in its throat. "I made preparations."

Dozens of vines shot out from the nearby forest, wrapping Khashair from head to foot.

An effort of will sent corruption out of his body in a wave, shattering the spell and rotting the vines to mush. Beside him, Gomo burned the vines attempting to wrap him up with hellfire.

Khashair turned to face the overseer. "Is that the extent of your preparations?"

More vines came rushing in.

This time Gomo dealt with them all, freeing Khashair to focus on the overseer. Using the power of the bile running through pipes under his feet, he sent tendrils of corrupt ether into the overseer's undead body.

Accelerated decay reduced the host to nothing in seconds.

Before the demon spirit had a chance to escape, Khashair wrapped it in dark chains, binding it in place.

"The vines seem to have lost their enthusiasm for the fight," Gomo said.

Khashair glanced back. Lines of ash ran from them to the forest, giving mute testimony to the effectiveness of Gomo's magic.

"Well done. I'm pleased I didn't kill you."

Leaving the demon dwarf to watch for any further shenanigans, Khashair strode over to the struggling spirit. "Save your energy. A weak spirit like you has no hope of breaking my binding."

"What do you want?"

"Knowledge. Specifically, where I can find all your cells and how best to contact them."

"They won't serve you. My humans are loyal to the archbishop."

Khashair smiled. "None of them have even seen the archbishop. I doubt I'll have any trouble convincing them that I'm the one they really serve. Now, no more distractions. I'm going to take the information I need from your spirit directly. Resist if you like, but know it will only make the process more painful."

Had there been anyone around to hear them, no doubt the spirit's screams would have sent a chill down their spine. To its credit, the minor demon did manage to slow Khashair's magic by nearly two seconds. Unfortunately, he ended up using too much power, snuffing out the spirit in the process.

He watched the last wisps of demonic essence vanish, to be absorbed into whatever hell vomited the spirit out. A bit of a waste, but Khashair had his own contacts in the Horned One's hell should he need to summon a demon.

"Now what?" Gomo asked.

"Now I send a summons to all the cells in the area and we wait at the meeting place for them to arrive. Once we have our first batch of volunteers, we move on to the next group."

"You make it sound simple. The real archbishop isn't just going to stand around and let you destroy everything she's built."

"I hope you're right. Another confrontation will give me a chance to destroy her. Having such a powerful enemy hiding in the background doing who knows what to interfere with my plans makes me uneasy."

Khashair shaped the ether like he saw in the demon's mind, matched it to the faces of the cult leaders, and blasted the summons out. They'd need time to gather, but soon a hundred or so fresh recruits would join his cause. As armies went, hardly the most impressive, but it would be a start.

———

Fane stood in Beastmaster's underground scrying chamber and forced ether into the crystal ball until she feared it might shatter. No matter how much energy she used, the mithril amulet refused to reveal itself. Only half a day had passed and yet somehow Khashair had managed to elude her. At least she'd warned her overseers of the danger. Not that she imagined they'd have a chance against the overmage, but at least they'd have the best possible chance of victory, however slim that might be.

At last she released the ether with a little snarl. Hate it as she might, Fane had to accept that, for the moment, her prey had escaped.

She smiled at her own arrogance. Calling Khashair her prey felt a bit like a wolf calling a tiger its prey. Until she figured out his secrets, she had no choice but to avoid a direct confrontation. Anything else would be suicide. And Fane hadn't survived this long only to die now.

A tremor ran through the ether and she staggered a step. One of her overseers had been destroyed. It didn't take a genius to know who did it either.

Fane hurried back to the crystal ball and this time focused on the spot where she sensed the overseer die. In a forest clearing she found Khashair and Gomo along with the remains of the demon spirit's host.

She pulled back and studied the area. Huge farms filled sheltered valleys. A placid river ran through the center of the valley and a safe distance from any flooding sat a modest town. She didn't know the name of the place, but this had to be Holden Province. Building her followers here had been a challenge as most people found the peaceful life soothing. Angry firebrands were in short supply. Still, if she remembered right, they'd managed around a hundred cultists in a dozen cells over the last decade.

Fane wanted to warn them, but she was as much a stranger to them as Khashair. She shook her head and released the ether. That group was lost. She didn't like it, but she did accept the truth.

Her larger force in Oceanus Province was another matter. Damned if she'd give them up so easily. Her hope had been to observe Khashair when he fought the overseers, but if she had no reliable way to find him, that wouldn't work.

Reaching out to her surviving overseer Fane said, "Order your cells to disperse. Warn them of a fraud archbishop who wants to lead them into a trap. Tell them to stay hidden until you contact them personally. When you're done, retreat to my citadel and wait for further instructions in the secure storage room in the basement."

As you command, Mistress.

Good, once her final overseer had done its job, there'd be nothing left for Khashair to steal. Let's see how far he got with a hundred recruits drawn from the most peaceful province in the empire.

It should make for an amusing diversion at least. And when Beastmaster returned with the information she needed to kill Khashair, the real fun would begin.

CHAPTER 8

Beastmaster never would've guessed that the Black Iron Empire was an archipelago, but having flown over three islands on his journey to Khashair's citadel, the truth became very obvious. He'd seen some interesting sights on his journey as well. Aside from some decidedly sketchy stone bridges and floating pillars, the only thing connecting the islands were the black iron pipes through which Black Bile still ran. He knew they remained active because the occasional leak left puddles of the stuff here and there.

On the plus side—if you could call it that—the land was already so dead that the bile didn't cause any damage no matter how much leaked out. He considered his maze as dangerous a place as you could find, but this place had to be the most lifeless. The only sign of movement he'd seen so far was a pack of four-legged demons he flew over a couple hours ago. They looked up at him as he passed, but tried nothing aggressive.

The fact that they couldn't fly he felt sure played a big part in that. The average demon weak enough to be summoned also tended to be stupid and aggressive. Some of Beastmaster's pets were smarter than the dumbest demons.

He shook his head and powered on.

Another hour of flying brought him within sight of the stone and black iron citadel. Someone had smashed it to ruins. Two of the four outer walls had fallen and the top floors of the main keep were so much rubble scattered around the courtyard. Not a terribly auspicious sign. The damage would also make searching a pain.

He'd hoped to make a quick end to his mission here, but it looked like he was doomed to disappointment.

Beastmaster landed in the courtyard as close as the rubble would allow to the still-standing portion of the keep. There were hints of a door concealed by the fallen stone, but even someone of his stature would have no hope of reaching it.

He smiled and with a mental command brought his pet squirrel out of his pocket. She sniffed and shied away from the ruin.

"I know it doesn't smell good, but you still have to go inside. Don't worry, it'll be safer than last time."

Her squeak sounded disbelieving.

"I know, but it's got to be done." He drove a thread of ether into her tiny brain, linking them.

With the spell in place, the squirrel became his puppet. Another thread linked their sight. Beastmaster set her down and closed his own eyes to avoid getting a headache from the double vision.

He sent her into the rubble. His pet clambered over broken stone, leapt jutting shards of black iron, and generally did whatever she had to in order to advance. At the squirrel's painfully slow pace it took most of half an hour to finally reach an open space inside the fortress. Not that there was much to see—a black tile entryway, black walls, and some fallen decoration crushed by stones.

And he thought his tunnels could be dreary. This place made Fane's citadel feel positively welcoming. His pet scurried around, checking down partially collapsed halls and crushed rooms for anything interesting. She found nothing and he finally willed her back to a set of stairs up to the next floor.

The path was mercifully clear of rubble and she reached the second-floor landing without issue. Alas, the door was shut and the gap between it and the floor too narrow for even his pet to squeeze through. Happily, there was plenty of room for Beastmaster to go and join her. He ordered her to stay where she was and disconnected their minds.

With his vision restored, Beastmaster spent a few minutes checking the fortress for wards and defenses. There were probably plenty of them at one time, but now nothing remained. The damage had broken the delicate spells. That was one good thing about it anyway.

Becoming one with the ether, he appeared on the second-floor landing an instant later. His pet climbed up his leg and perched in her usual spot on his shoulder. She squeaked at him.

"I told you it was safe, not pleasant. I need to concentrate now, so back in my pocket."

She scampered and disappeared into his robe. She'd stay there until he called her back.

Now. Time to see what he could see.

He pushed hard and the door opened a foot before hitting something heavy. It looked like a fallen timber. No way was he pushing that aside.

Oh well, it wasn't his door after all.

An ethereal whip sliced the door in half and he pushed the top half the rest of the way open. Beyond it lay a huge library. No doubt all the secrets of the overmages were hidden here. Pity the floor above had come crashing down, ruining everything inside. He saw nothing salvageable.

What a waste.

Even worse, it meant he'd have to fly to the next citadel. Hopefully he'd find that one in better shape.

"First things first," he muttered.

He settled down on a clear section of the floor and retrieved something to eat from his pack. A ham-and-cheese sandwich wasn't the fanciest meal in the world, but it would sustain him for half a day. Sometimes Beastmaster thought Fane had the right idea, transforming into an undead. Not that he'd choose the same form as her—too many limitations—but not having to eat and sleep might be nice.

He took a bite of food. The salty ham, crusty bread, and creamy cheese made a delightful combination. Convenient or not, he'd miss food too much to become undead. Besides, it would make working with his pets far harder. They all hated Fane and her overseers.

Half an hour to eat lunch followed by a two-hour nap had Beastmaster back in tip-top shape. Lucky for him the next citadel was a shorter flight away. Four or five hours at most.

He became one with the ether and appeared where he started earlier. Only now he wasn't alone. The trio of four-legged demons he saw earlier faced him from about twenty feet way. They carried lances, had ugly, fur-covered lower bodies, and equally ugly, red-skinned humanoid bodies on top.

Beastmaster hated demons. Their flesh was to unstable to make useful raw materials and most of the ones weak enough to be summoned easily were dumb as stumps. This group looked just as stupid up close as they had from a distance, but maybe they could at least tell him if the next citadel was intact. If it was in as bad a shape as this one, he'd try somewhere else.

"I've got a couple questions," Beastmaster said. "Answer them and I'll let you go."

One of the demons roared and thrust its lance at him.

Chains of ether wrapped it up and stopped it a foot from his chest.

Roaring and yanking with all its might, the demon tried to free its weapon to no avail. Instead, Beastmaster jerked it free of the demon's grasp, spun it around, and drove it through the monster's chest.

It promptly dissolved into a puddle of black goo.

The other two demons stared at him. Most people did that when they realized he wasn't actually a twelve-year-old boy. Though if they'd thought that's what he was, they were even stupider than he first believed.

"Can either of you speak?" he asked in Imperial but received no reply. "Hmm. Either you can't or you don't speak that language."

He tried again in Demonic.

Their eyes widened and the one on the left said, "We can speak. What do you wish to know, Little Master?"

Beastmaster grinned. Little Master. He quite liked the sound of that. And even better, the survivors seemed inclined to be reasonable. Never what you expected where demons were concerned, but a nice surprise all the same.

"Is the nearest citadel in the same shape as this one?" The demons looked at each other as if uncertain what he meant. Beastmaster pointed east. "That way, about three hundred miles."

The demons brightened at once. Not that anyone would actually want to see a smiling demon. Too many fangs and the black gums, not to mention rotten breath, made Beastmaster wish he'd waited a little longer on his lunch.

"Apologies, but that one is in worse shape than this one. We have traveled most of this broken land and found only three intact citadels." The demon pointed northwest. "The nearest is that way, many days' run from here. Forgive me, human measurements are a mystery to me."

Beastmaster waved a dismissive hand and pulled out his book. Northwest. Hmmm. That one was actually way closer to where he arrived than Khashair's had been. All that time and energy wasted for nothing.

"You've been very helpful," Beastmaster said. "Feel free to go on your way. And if you could tell any other demons you meet about me, it should save me some aggravation later on."

"We will spread the word, Little Master. Thank you for sparing us."

The demons trotted out one of the shattered walls and were soon gone from sight. As demons went, they'd turned out to be quite decent. If the other nasty things that lived in the area were as easy to dominate as them, the Black Iron Empire might be a fun playground after all.

CHAPTER 9

Cardinal Rufious paced in his office. He had a stack of paperwork a foot tall that needed his attention. It had been building since the mission to reclaim their easternmost fortress departed. He found himself unable to concentrate on it for more than fifteen minutes at a time. That was a first for him. Usually, he had no trouble walling off his many concerns to focus on the day-to-day needs of the church. But something about this mess struck him as different from the usual chaos he dealt with.

And not just the attack on the fortress. The business with the demon that attacked them and the crazy monster that slaughtered her way through First Circle, all of it seemed connected. He just didn't fully understand how.

And he needed to. The church was in this up to their necks. Samaritan or Bellator or whatever the fallen White Knight wanted to call himself made it impossible for the church to just leave it to the army.

Maybe some fresh air would clear his mind.

Rufious pushed the door open and made the walk silently to the main chapel and out into the afternoon sunlight. Maybe there was something in his expression, but the priest on duty offered only a silent nod of respect.

The cold winter air slapped him alert. Spring might be coming, but right now it felt a long ways away. He walked down the steps with no particular destination in mind.

A small figure came running his way from the barracks. Looked like one of the squires training to be White Knights. And the aviary was behind the barracks. Maybe the boy had a message. Out of habit he offered a prayer to The One God that it was from Valen. Some news, even bad news, might help him to settle down.

"Cardinal Rufious?" the dark-eyed youth asked. He had a small message scroll clutched in his right hand.

"Yes. Is that for me?" Rufious sounded calm at least, despite his racing heart.

"Yes, Your Grace. From Knight Captain Valen. It arrived just this moment."

Rufious took the scroll and offered his most benevolent smile. "Thank you, Squire. Back to your training now."

The boy bowed and ran back the way he'd come. Ah, to be so energetic and free of concerns.

He retreated to his office. Whatever the scroll had to say, he didn't want to read it outside where anyone might walk up to him and catch a glimpse.

The brisk walk soon saw him settled back into his chair. A deep breath steadied his nerves, a little anyway. This was what he'd been waiting for, damn it. Stop acting like a child and read the cursed report!

He unrolled the little scroll and frowned. The artifact was gone, the White Knights were dead, and Gaius seemed confident that something other than the spider monster had killed them. Rufious had been certain there would be bad news and he wasn't disappointed. This was about as bad as he could have expected. Even worse, there were no clues about where the artifact or the wizard had gone.

Valen wanted new orders. Rufious wished he had a clue what to tell him.

Maybe Septimus would have an idea.

He smiled at his optimism. The pope had his talents, but somehow Rufious doubted sorting this mess out was within the pope's reach. Or his for that matter.

Rufious shrugged and once more marched out of his office and down the hall, this time in the opposite direction. He tried the office first with little optimism and sure enough found the door locked. Rufious used his key just to make sure and nodded at the empty room. Hopefully he wasn't drunk or with the nuns. Though of the two, the nuns would be better. Sobering Septimus up always took ages.

He knocked on the bedroom door without pressing his ear to it first. The last time Rufious did that he swore he'd never do it again. Septimus liked to talk dirty and Rufious had no desire to hear it.

After far too long a wait, the door opened and a robed but otherwise naked Septimus glared at him. "You have the most dreadful timing. I'm in the middle of training our newest arrival. Can't the current emergency wait until tomorrow?"

"We got a report from Valen and the news isn't good."

"Shit!" He looked back over his shoulder and shouted into the dark room. "Don't get dressed. I'll be back in a few minutes."

Without another word Septimus led the way to his office. Rufious did his best not to look closely at the pope's flabby figure outlined by the too-tight robe. He'd never looked into the nuns' salaries, but whatever it was, they deserved a raise.

When the office door closed, Septimus turned to face him. "How bad?"

Rufious told him everything. "Valen wants orders and I have no idea what to tell him. My inclination is to issue a recall and abandon the fortress. There's no point manning it now that the artifact is gone. Sounds like they had no idea where to look for the artifact or the wizard, assuming it was him that took it."

"Go talk to someone at the palace. I assume their people sent a message as well."

Rufious shrugged. "Valen didn't say, but that's reasonable. Under the circumstances, I believe I'll go now. Do you have any particular thoughts on the matter?"

"We don't know enough for me to have thoughts. Whatever you decide, I'll back you. Now get going."

Rufious nodded and set out for the palace. Hopefully someone there would have a plan since he certainly didn't.

———

Alexandra sat across from Cardinal Rufious, her expression neutral, and in full Iron Princess mode. They were meeting in one of the spare lounges kept for just this sort of discussion. No one wanted it to get out that the church and palace were having high-level meetings on even a semi-regular basis.

That said, she'd been expecting to hear from the church from the moment the message arrived from the head alchemist on site. The knight commander must have sent his own message at nearly the same time for the cardinal to have shown up so soon. Hopefully he had some new information to share.

"You asked for this meeting," Alexandra said. "I'm all ears."

"May I assume you got a report from your people at the fortress as well?"

"We did. Nothing in it made me happy. I've already ordered the Fourth Legion back to their barracks."

"Wise decision. The pope is inclined to abandon the fortress for now and bring our knights back to the capital. Unless you can offer a better suggestion?"

Alexandra leaned back in her hard wooden chair. Did he really know nothing more? It seemed impossible, yet she sensed no deception in him.

"I don't. In fact, I planned to do the same thing with the alchemists. We may as well have them travel back together." Time to try the straightforward approach. "The crown is at a loss. I have no idea how best to proceed in this matter. Both the wizard and the artifact could be anywhere by now. Does the church have any idea where we might search next?"

Rufious leaned forward, fingers steepled. "I appreciate your honesty. Unfortunately, we haven't a clue. I came in the hope that you did. It seems we're both in the same boat, at the mercy of the current and sailing into the dark."

Alexandra nodded. He'd just confirmed her worst-case scenario. "I intend to put all imperial forces on alert with orders to report anything, no matter how small. I suggest you do the same."

"Agreed. Unless events require otherwise, I suggest we meet again next God's Day at the church. That will draw less attention than me coming to the palace."

Alexandra stood and held out her hand. "Agreed."

They shook and Rufious headed back to the church.

When he'd gone she slumped in the chair. Having to wait on the enemy was every general's least favorite thing to do. She wanted to attack. Or even defend. At least then she'd have an enemy in front of her. Just waiting made her nervous. That lunatic wizard might be up to anything.

Though whatever he was up to, she knew it would be a nightmare for the empire.

CHAPTER 10

Fane strode down the tunnel that led to Beastmaster's flesh pits. She carried a skin of water and a pouch filled with jerky. A few days had passed since Beastmaster left and she figured the prisoner must be in need of sustenance. She still had no idea what she was going to do with the man. And the more she thought about it, the less she understood her reasons for keeping him alive.

She made a right and entered the cavern. A musty, animal stink lay over everything, making Fane glad she didn't actually have to breathe. The prisoner stared up at her from his pit. The White Knight's hair had grown long and scraggly. His cheeks were sunken and his eyes red.

Despite drinking a cure all not that long ago, he didn't look terribly healthy.

"How long are you going to keep me here?" he asked.

Fane tossed him the skin and pouch. "I haven't decided yet. Your former colleague's body has been taken over by the spirit of a long-dead wizard. I spared you so you might offer me insight into Samaritan's way of thinking. But if he's no longer the one in charge, it would probably be safe enough to kill you."

"Bellator has been possessed? How did that happen? He has the strongest will of any man I've ever known."

Fane shrugged and sat on the edge of the pit. "I don't know exactly how it happened. Perhaps he let Khashair have his body willingly. Despite working with him for several years, I really know little about him. Do you think he might have allowed himself to become host to a powerful, evil spirit?"

The prisoner scratched his beard. Fane didn't know why she was wasting her time talking to the man. Maybe because she had no one else to talk to and she needed to get her thoughts sorted out. Having to flee left her in a dark place mentally. The idea that there was someone on this miserable world she needed to fear enraged her.

"Bellator might have agreed if the spirit had the power and knowledge necessary to carry out his revenge. When I looked in his eyes before he sent me crashing into this sinkhole, I saw madness burning there. I fear he may have completely lost his way."

Fane laughed. "I could have told you that. Do you think he has any attachment left in this world? Anything I might use to break the link between him and Khashair's spirit?"

"I don't know. I would be willing to try and reach him, though I might well die for my trouble. If there's any chance I might succeed, it's worth the risk."

Fane stood. She seriously doubted Samaritan felt strongly enough about a man he tried to kill not so long ago that it would break the bond between him and Khashair. Perhaps if she got truly desperate, she might try it in the hopes that a momentary distraction would give her an opening to loose a killing spell.

"I will consider your words." With that she stalked off back to the scrying chamber. Enough time should have passed for the cultists to have gathered to meet Khashair in his guise as the archbishop.

A few minutes later found her once again with the tips of her fingers resting on the smooth crystal. One good thing about the meeting: she didn't have to worry about locating Khashair. Several of the cultists should have the bronze medallions she'd enchanted to make contacting them easier. Honing in on those would be simple.

Seconds later she found her consciousness looking down at a gathering of perhaps eighty people, mostly men, none prosperous. Fane didn't think she'd ever actually seen a gathering of those chosen to serve in her name. If this lot was the best the overseer could find, she didn't know why she wasted her time. They wouldn't last five minutes in a fight.

On the plus side, Khashair wouldn't gain much from stealing them. Assuming he didn't change them into bile zombies. And if he was going to do that, he could have simply kidnapped anyone he ran into.

She shrugged and shifted her view. No sign of Khashair and the demon yet, but they'd be along soon enough.

People trickled in until she counted ninety-seven. A familiar figure in a white cloak entered, followed by Gomo. The bastard hadn't even bothered to change out of Samaritan's filthy uniform. Lazy or arrogant, she couldn't decide.

A few people muttered, no doubt recognizing the White Knight uniform. She was surprised none of them tried to bolt at the sight of it.

Khashair raised his hands. "Thank you for coming, everyone. My name is Khashair, better known to you as the archbishop. You may be wondering why I'm finally speaking to you in person. The time has come at last to strike at the empire. To cast them down and build something better. Powerful weapons and armor have been prepared for those of you with the courage to take them up. Those who fight will be given first choice of rewards when the empire falls, but even if you lack the courage to take up a sword, the world will have need of your talents. I'm counting on all of you, my loyal followers, to help me make our dream a reality."

The man gave a good speech, Fane wouldn't deny that. She doubted she would have done as well. Of course, she had no practice ruling an empire. Pretty speech or not, she'd heard all she cared to.

After returning her awareness to her body, she conjured a sphere of negative energy the size of her head. Those were her cultists and if she couldn't have them, no one would.

———

K hashair couldn't help smiling at the number of cultists that showed up for the meeting. He would've been happy to get half of them, but unless the information he took from the overseer was wrong, all but a handful were here. Granted, they didn't look terribly impressive in their dirty tunics and scuffed boots, but he hadn't expected legionnaires. They looked healthy and strong enough to swing a sword, and most importantly, survive what he planned to do to them.

Black iron weapons would make up some of the difference between them and actual soldiers and his potions would do the rest.

"I'm not impressed," Gomo muttered from behind him.

"You don't need to be. They're sufficient for a start. Hopefully we can upgrade later. Now be quiet and keep your distance. I'm not sure they're ready to meet a demon yet."

Gomo grunted and moved back near the entrance to a barn that served as their meeting place before turning invisible. At least invisible to anyone unable to see magic. Khashair stepped forward, raised his hands for quiet, and began the speech he'd prepared. Speaking to his soldiers was something he did on a regular basis back in his old home, so the job came naturally.

When he reached the first pause for cheers, he sensed something magical.

He got no more warning before a small portal opened. A white hand holding a head-sized ball of darkness emerged and dropped the ball in the middle of his new recruits.

Khashair conjured, quickly wrapping the sphere in an ethereal bubble.

It exploded with enough force to shatter his sphere.

Luckily for him, that reduced its power enough that most of the cultists survived. Though from the look of them, most of the survivors probably wished they hadn't.

The portal, along with the hand of the true archbishop, had already vanished.

It seemed he'd have to take greater care to shield himself when he was beyond the wards of his storehouse.

I doubt she found you. Some of the cultists carry enchanted amulets that allow her to speak to them. That's likely how she located you so easily.

"It didn't occur to you to mention that sooner?"

You told me to remain silent if I didn't wish to be destroyed. I also didn't think of it until she struck.

Khashair kept his expression calm even as he seethed inside. Samaritan had a point, damn him. "You have my permission to speak if you have something useful to say."

He felt Samaritan's amusement even though he chose to remain silent. There was a hint of cruelty in that amusement that Khashair found familiar. Perhaps he and Samaritan shared an ancient ancestor.

Putting his host out of his mind, Khashair turned to the groaning cultists. "You see how much our enemies fear you, my friends? They want to destroy you before you become strong enough to threaten them. But we're not going to let that happen. Some of you wear my amulets, that may be how our enemies figured out where we were. Leave them here and we'll go to my sanctuary."

Three men and a woman dropped bronze amulets on the ground. The survivors followed him outside and Khashair opened a portal back to the storehouse. Or more specifically the area outside the tower.

They all eyed the ethereal portal with trepidation. And it was rather disconcerting, he was honest enough to admit that. "Steel yourselves, my friends, and step into your new lives as conquerors."

One of the men finally got up the nerve and marched through. That encouraged the others and soon only Khashair and Gomo remained behind.

"Didn't think they'd have the guts," Gomo said. "But the real test will come when they face a wall of imperial steel."

"Don't worry about that. I have ways of stiffening their spines."

He didn't add that the process would also remove most of their human conscience as well. No need to point that out until after they drank the potions.

Khashair and Gomo went through last and emerged at the rear of the gawping peasants. The ruin wasn't the nicest place to find yourself but it was safe enough.

"Have no fear," Khashair said. "Though it doesn't look like much, this is my temporary base and perfectly safe for those loyal to me. Come along and I will show you the arsenal that will destroy the empire."

The cultists murmured among themselves, but so far no one had found the nerve to ask any questions. That suited him fine. A little bit of fear mingled with loyalty made it all the stronger.

He strode through the crowd, into the tower, and down to the basement. The cultists followed with a good deal less confidence. But they did follow. He'd been certain that at some point compulsion magic would be necessary. Whatever else, these were dedicated people. Probably more dedicated than any of his servants and soldiers from his old life.

In the armory the cultists stared at the statues and racks of weapons and armor with wide eyes. Khashair let them drink it all in as he went to the collection of potions covering a section of the wall. He had several hundred potions of mutagen, more than enough to enhance all his followers. Now to get them to drink one.

"My friends, before we get you geared up, there's one more matter to attend to. To become a force the empire will fear, you must become strong and tough." He held up a vial filled with golden liquid flecked with black. "One of these potions combined with the weapons and armor will make you a match for ten legionnaires."

One of the cultists finally worked up the nerve to speak. "Are they safe?"

"Perfectly." Khashair popped the cork out of the vial he held and drank down the contents.

His magic neutralized the potion then he used a self-enhancement spell to make his muscles bulge and his skin grow as tough as leather. Khashair drew a dagger and pulled it across his forearm. The razor-sharp steel didn't bite in the least.

"See what you will become?"

They crowded forward now, eager to gain the power he offered.

"Steady, friends, there's enough for everyone. When you each have a vial, we'll drink together. A toast to the empire's destruction."

They cheered and he hurried to hand out a potion to each of them. Happily, no one felt the need to take an early sip. He didn't want anyone getting a sneak peek at what would actually happen when they drank the potion.

When they each had one, Khashair thrust a fist into the air. "Death to the Tiberian Empire!"

"Death!" they all roared before drinking as one.

A few seconds passed before the screaming began. The cultists all fell to the floor in a writhing heap as they moaned and twisted. All but one.

The sole cultist still holding a full vial stared at his fellows in utter horror.

"Well, this is unfortunate," Khashair said. "You really should have drunk with your fellows. It would have made things much simpler for you."

"What did you do to them? Why bring us here only to kill us?"

"Kill you?" Khashair shook his head. "I have no intention of killing my loyal followers. The problem is, unlike me, you are just ordinary men. A transformation of this magnitude is much harder for you than me. Rest assured, in a few hours, they will be back on their feet, stronger, faster, and tougher than any human on the planet. Will you drink and take your place at my side as one of the elites of the new world?"

The cultist looked at his still-writhing fellows and swallowed hard. "If I don't?"

Khashair smiled and tried to make it look unthreatening. "I told you before I brought you here that I had need of noncombatants as well. If you wish to serve me in such a role, that's perfectly fine. I bear you no ill will either way."

The man visibly relaxed then straightened, looked Khashair right in the eye, and drank. He collapsed a moment later to join the chorus of moans. It was rare to find a human with guts like that. He made a note of the man's appearance; the pale skin, red hair, and freckles should make him easy to pick out even after the transformation was complete.

"I doubted you'd be able to talk them into it." Gomo shimmered into view. "What does that potion really do?"

"Just what I told them."

Gomo raised a bushy eyebrow.

"Well, not just that. It also makes them totally obedient and removes their ability to know right from wrong. Now they will only know how to obey my orders."

"So you basically made them into zombies."

"On the contrary. They will retain their full intellect and will perform whatever task I give them to the best of their ability." Khashair shook his head. "We learned long ago the limits of the undead. They are tremendously useful in certain situations, but their stupidity and lack of flexibility make them far too limited for my taste. This potion is the best of both worlds. The brains of men and the loyalty of undead. We used them extensively in the Black Iron Empire."

"I'll bet. So what now?"

"They'll be most of a day recovering from the transformation. I intend to find the remaining overseer and collect more soldiers. Once that's done, it'll be time for a test."

"What sort of test?" Gomo asked.

"A raid. We're going to burn down the church, kill the pope and any other churchmen, and slaughter the imperial family."

CHAPTER 11

The imperial dragon ship felt kind of empty to Joran without Alexandra and the Iron Guards aboard. On the one hand it was nice to have the extra room, on the other, everyone looked at him to take charge. Not that there was much to take charge of since they were traveling across a peaceful section of the empire and as far as Joran knew there were no dangers that might knock them out of the sky this time. Of course, he'd thought that before and the geomancers proved him wrong.

He spent the first day standing on the bridge trying to pretend he had any idea what the crew was doing. By the end of the day, he had a pretty good idea how everything worked. Even better, the captain made it clear that he didn't need Joran to stand there and watch them. If there was a problem, someone would come and get him.

That suited Joran fine. It also allowed him to focus on what he really wanted to do this trip which was learn as much about magic as possible from Grub. They were currently seated on the floor of the hold facing each other. Grub was doing something magical while Joran watched the ether to see exactly how.

Unfortunately, the amount of ether involved confused his eyes and he couldn't really tell anything. The occasional clash of Mia's and Stoneheart's practice weapons didn't help his concentration. Mia said she needed to stay in practice and Stoneheart seemed eager to spar with her.

"Stop," Joran said at last. "There's too much going on with your spell. Can't we start with something simpler?"

Grub scratched his beard with his new hand. "This is the simplest illusion spell I know. Maybe you just don't have a knack for this kind of magic. Not every wizard can do every type of magic. Illusion probably isn't your thing. We'll try something else."

On the far side of the hold the clanging stopped when Mia sent Stoneheart's blunt wooden axe flying.

"Ha!" Mia said. "Three in a row."

Stoneheart scrubbed a hand across his face as he stalked over to pick up his practice weapon. "I can't believe a girl young enough to be my great-granddaughter can take me three in a row. It's not natural."

"Don't feel too bad, Stoneheart," Joran said. "I doubt there are a handful of people in the empire that can fight on even footing with Mia."

"We'll see. Fourth time's the charm."

Joran grinned at his determination. Stoneheart didn't quit for anything. He admired that about the dwarf.

When he turned back, Grub had placed three knuckle-sized pebbles on the floor.

"I know this game. One of them has a pea under it, right?"

Grub snorted. "Hardly. Since illusion isn't your thing, we'll try telekinesis. As far as magic is concerned, this is about as totally opposite as you can get. Ready?"

Joran nodded and shifted his vision back to the ether. This time, instead of a mass of ether writhing in front of him, he saw only a single braid with a three-pronged hand at the end. The hand opened, clamped on to the central stone, and moved it beside the right-hand one. This looked doable. He understood everything he saw.

Whether he could duplicate it or not was another matter.

The spell vanished and Grub asked, "What do you think?"

"I think I'll try it. This spell at least made a certain amount of sense to me."

Grub nodded. "If the ethereal construct is clear to you, that's an excellent sign. Try to do what I did. Take your time. No one's trying to kill us today, so speed isn't essential."

Joran took a deep breath to settle his nerves. He'd been dabbling at magic for a little while now. A simple experiment like this shouldn't make him so nervous.

Right, to business. Grub's spell had resembled braided rope. Joran pictured three strands of ether as big around as his pinky. When they appeared, his chest tightened and his breathing grew shallow.

That was new.

"Don't add any more ether," Grub said. "You're right at your limit. Transform the end into a claw."

Joran focused. Careful not to draw any more power to him, he formed a three-pronged claw out of the end of the rope.

Now for the stone.

Painfully, slowly, he opened the claw just enough to grab the left-hand stone. He clamped down and tried to lift it.

The pebble felt like a boulder at first, but it did finally shift, lifting a fraction off the deck and sliding over beside the other two. When he dropped it, Joran let out a gasp. He hadn't been this tired after fighting the giant serpent.

"Well done, Lord Den Cade," Grub said. "Telekinesis is clearly a type of magic you have a talent for."

Joran nodded, not trusting himself to speak yet. When his heart had slowed to something approaching normal, he said, "Thanks. Is it supposed to be this hard?"

"Unfortunately, yes. But the more you practice, the easier it'll get. Eventually you'll be able to lift bigger and bigger objects and your control will grow more refined until you reach your personal limit."

"What's that?"

"Every wizard has a limit, a point past which you can't push. You'll know it when you reach that point. The pain will be such that you can think of nothing beyond ending it."

"Any more good news?"

Grub grinned. "Not at the moment. Do you want to try a different sort of spell?"

Joran laughed and shook his head. "Not today. All I want now is food and a nap."

"That's good. Understanding how much you can handle is important for a wizard. When you're ready let me know and we can try some elemental magic."

Intrigued despite his exhaustion Joran asked, "What's that?"

"Just what it sounds like, magic that lets you influence the elements: earth, fire, wind, and water. We won't get into the powers of life and death, too complicated and way outside my area of expertise. Wind is also one I can't use."

"Why not wind?" Joran asked.

"As a geomancer, earth magic is my specialty and wind magic is directly opposed to it. Like I said earlier, there are some types of magic that some wizards just can't use."

"Fascinating. Has someone codified all this knowledge? Perhaps in the dwarven archive?"

Grub shook his head. "My people hate magic and geomancers along with it. What I know—in the grand scheme of things, it isn't much—I learned by word of mouth from my mentor, just as he did from his."

"That's horribly inefficient."

Grub shrugged. "Better than nothing."

Joran couldn't argue with that. He stood. "Thank you for the lesson. Shall we pick up here tomorrow?"

"Sure. It's not like I have anything else to do on this ship. And it feels good to pass on what I learned, even if I am passing it on to a human instead of a fellow geomancer."

"Maybe when our current troubles are over, we can see about doing something for your fellows. The empire owes you a debt for all you've done. I'll do my best to see it gets paid back."

"I won't hold my breath."

Joran smiled at the retort. Typical Grub and he wasn't wrong. The emperor might be his future father-in-law, but he certainly wouldn't act on just Joran's request.

But that was a problem for later.

"Mia. I'm going for a bite to eat. Do you want to come or are you going to abuse Stoneheart some more?"

His soulmate grinned and tossed her practice sword to Stoneheart. "I'm starving. Five in a row's enough for today."

"Five in a row," Stoneheart muttered and shook his head.

Joran felt bad for him, but at least Mia seemed happy. Hopefully a good meal and a nap would restore Joran's strength enough to practice his new spell at least once more before bed. He wanted to build up as much magical strength as possible before they arrived.

It might end up being the difference between life and death.

CHAPTER 12

Beastmaster felt like he'd been reading forever. When he arrived, he'd found the largely intact citadel empty save for a smashed golem surrounded by a heap of broken black iron. Not that he was about to complain. Dealing with demons was a pain, even if the weak ones had no hope of hurting him. And golems weren't much better.

On the second floor he found another library, bigger than the ruined one he left. In it sat a catalogue written in those strange symbols that resisted his translation spell. When he tried again, they still resisted, but this time he forced the matter. If they ended up erased, he'd be no worse off and he was sick of playing around here. Back home, Fane was probably having a fit that he hadn't returned yet.

Of course, since she was always having a fit about something, that would be no surprise.

To his delight, he got to read some of the catalogue before the symbols vanished. It gave him a starting place anyway. Of course, there were easily ten thousand books in the library, so even a starting place would only help so much.

In the end, what saved him from wasting a fair chunk of his

immortality was luck. Six books in he stumbled across one about the overmages, specifically one that talked about the training they gave their apprentices. Turned out, the reason they were so strong was that they knew how to draw on the power of the Black Bile from a distance. Basically, as long as the pipes flowed under their feet, they had access to unlimited power.

At the very least that explained why Khashair beat Fane. Unfortunately, there was no hint as to how they did it or how to stop them from doing it. No doubt that secret was only passed on by word of mouth. Still, combined with the atlas he found mapping the pipes, they could at least figure out how far Khashair's power reached.

Beastmaster hoped that would be enough to satisfy Fane. For the time being, he'd had his fill of this miserable place. He still planned to come back at some point to explore, but on his timetable, not hers.

After a long sigh, he added the journal to the atlas in his satchel. Time to go home.

He retreated to the courtyard then out beyond the walls. One thing the overmages had a knack for was warding their citadels. This one had the most powerful anti-teleportation ward he'd ever encountered. Probably powered by the bile as well.

Once clear, Beastmaster became one with the ether and a moment later found himself back in his throne room. Or what he thought of as his throne room. It was really just a big chair with a button that opened the trapdoor leading to the maze.

The door slammed open and Fane stalked in. "Tell me you have good news."

He winced. "I have news. How good it is, you'll have to decide for yourself."

Beastmaster explained about the bile.

"Stop!" Fane stared at him, her eyes glowing brighter than

usual. "You're telling me Khashair can call on the bile's power without holding it in his hand? How is that possible? I can't do it."

"The book didn't say." Beastmaster dug the journal out of his satchel and offered it to her. "It's probably one of the overmages' big secrets. Anyway, all we have to do is stay beyond the pipes, and we'll be fine. Without the power boost, I doubt he'd be a match for you."

"Of course he wouldn't be. But we'd have to leave behind everything we've built here. And if the source of the bile is somewhere near the pipes, we'll never reach it."

"Do you know what the source is?" He'd been wondering for a while, but having seen firsthand what happened in the Black Iron Empire, he felt like he needed to know.

Fane glared at him but Beastmaster didn't flinch. He was tired of all her secrets.

"The source is a dragon, the most powerful creature on the planet. I plan to wake it and then enslave it after the beast exhausts itself. But if I can't reach it, that will never happen."

"Is that such a terrible thing?" Beastmaster dared ask.

When she shot him a particularly hard glare he hastened to add, "I mean, you don't even need to wake it to seize its power. You just need to figure out how Khashair wields the bile's power and you could do the same thing. Then it's just a matter of extending the pipe network all over the world and you'll be unstoppable everywhere. As long as it's nighttime anyway."

Her expression softened and he knew she was finally thinking about what he said rather than getting ready to dismiss it out of hand.

"There may be something to what you say. I've been thinking about it off and on since I learned the fate of the Black Iron Empire. When Lord Sur returns, I don't want to hand him an entirely dead world. If, on the other hand, I hand him a world where his power was even greater, he might at last teach me the secret of becoming a true arcane lord."

Beastmaster nodded. He'd be happy to encourage her in this line of thinking. If all the animals ended up dead, he'd have nothing to experiment on.

He knew little about the arcane lords that brought his long-dead master to this world, but from what he picked up during his apprenticeship, he gathered they were the most powerful wizards around. The way Fane worshipped her master told Beastmaster everything he needed to know about how powerful they were. Fane certainly wouldn't worship anybody that didn't totally outclass her.

"So," Beastmaster said. "How do we figure out Khashair's technique? I mean, there's got to be some trick to it, right? I haven't actually seen him cast. Did you notice what he did?"

She grimaced, baring her fangs. "No. At the time, I was busy trying to stay in one piece. We're going to need to arrange a test for the good overmage. Something that will require him to really exert that power of his."

Her expression smoothed into a smile.

Beastmaster found it even scarier than her scowl.

———

Khashair snarled his psyche back to his body. He'd been searching for hours, trying in vain to find the second overseer and the knowledge it held. Nothing filled with so much corruption should be able to hide from him. Of course, he'd had no luck finding the female vampire either, though given her magical ability, that came as less of a surprise.

He stood and turned his attention to his new troops. The cultists were starting to come out of their transformations. Another hour or so should have them on their feet. He'd hoped to add another hundred to his force before attacking Tiber, but without the overseer's knowledge, he had no way to find them. Unless you knew who they were, the cultists all appeared to be nothing but ordinary people.

"No luck?" Gomo asked.

He growled a little then shook his head. "No."

"She probably ordered the creature into hiding after you destroyed the last one. The woman isn't stupid."

"Pity you're right. Stupid opponents are so much easier to deal with. I'll just have to send a few more golems than I first intended. Combined with our magic, it should still be plenty to get the job done."

Gomo looked at him, head slightly cocked. "Don't misunderstand, I love a bit of random destruction as much as the next demon, but is there a greater point to attacking the capital when you have no hope of administering it?"

"It's a demonstration of my power as well as a way to decapitate the empire's leadership. Without a central command, the provinces will be reduced to following the orders of their lord governors. The generals of each legion will be forced to act on their own. It will be chaos."

If you need more soldiers, there are rebels among the dwarves that might join you even if you don't pretend to be the archbishop. They just want the leaders in Dwarfhome dead. Also, why don't you seek out the cultists with amulets? You could probably find a few new recruits that way.

Finally, some useful suggestions. "I'm going to try a few more things. Keep an eye on the troops and tap my shoulder when they're awake."

"As you wish."

Khashair returned to his spot on the floor and sent his psychic body flying again. He pictured the amulets the cultists carried and soon found himself in the barn where they met. Studying their magical signature told him all he needed to know to locate the rest.

Soon he found himself flying east toward the coast. When he finally stopped, he cursed the universe. A pile of six amulets sat in a heap on a soggy island in the middle of a swamp. She must have figured he'd come looking and ordered the cultists to discard them.

This archbishop was starting to get on his nerves.

Try the dwarves. She might not have warned them yet.

Khashair seriously doubted that, but it never hurt to be thorough.

Turning his focus north he sensed only a single, weak signature. Quick as thought, he flew to it. The amulet rested in the pocket of a fat dwarf who stood in front of a closed door. Beyond it sat a tired-looking man.

Titus! How did he end up here?

"You know that human?"

He's my only friend. Someone must have learned he was helping me and locked him up. We need to free him.

"There is no 'we.' I have no intention of wasting my time rescuing a single, useless man. Your friend can sit here until the end of time for all I care."

No!

Samaritan's consciousness surged up, trying to wrestle control of his psychic form. It was such a powerful effort that Khashair nearly didn't react in time.

Nearly.

With an effort of will, he pushed Samaritan back down into the background. Perhaps he had underestimated the strength of his partner. Destroying him might be more difficult than he first believed.

"I'll make you a bargain. Don't do that again and after we finish with Tiber, we'll deal with Dwarfhome next. We can free your friend in the process. Deal?"

The silence in his mind lingered far too long, but finally Samaritan responded. *Deal.*

A final psychic sweep of the area confirmed that the amulet held by the fat dwarf was the only one around. It seemed the vampire was more thorough than he'd hoped.

But no matter. He had sufficient forces to slaughter the imperial family and every churchman in Tiber.

Yes. They must suffer for what they did to my soulmate.

"I didn't forget. Slaying the pope and his subordinates is almost as important as eliminating the emperor and his family. Soon you will have your revenge and I will begin my conquest of this continent."

CHAPTER 13

The flight ended up taking less time than Joran feared. Only a week after leaving the capital, they were beginning the descent toward the empire's northwestern-most border fort. Not that they were going to land. The border forts didn't have nearly enough room in their courtyards for a dragon ship to set down.

No, when they got low enough it was a ride down in the gondola for Joran and his team. The prospect didn't even unnerve him anymore. What they may or may not find at the end of this mission, on the other hand, unnerved him a great deal. He'd been trying and failing to figure out how to confirm the dragon's presence without actually waking it up. Tiptoeing seemed an overly simplistic idea, but it was the only realistic one he'd had so far.

At least he'd gotten some magical practice in. Turned out, telekinesis was his best skill. After just five days, he'd gotten good enough to pull Mia's sword to his hand without feeling like passing out or throwing up afterwards. He also managed a tiny flame and a spark of lightning. Not exactly the most overwhelming of successes, but he already felt his power growing and, assuming they survived and made it back to Tiber, a future as a wizard seemed within his reach.

"Copper for your thoughts," Mia said as the pair made their way to the hold and waiting gondola.

Joran smiled at his soulmate. "Just thinking about everything that's happened on this flight and what the future might hold. Speaking of which, did Stoneheart ever get a win?"

"No, but he got close a couple times and showed me a few tendencies I have that need correcting. Fighting a skilled opponent able to match my speed could get me into trouble."

Joran's smile broadened. "If we find someone as fast and skilled as you, we'll all be in trouble. Hopefully such a person doesn't live in the Land of the Blood Drinkers."

"Why do they call it that anyway?"

"I never researched it. Since I doubt it's a nation of vampires, I have to assume there was some sort of religious or magical ritual involving drinking blood or something that looked like blood. Of course, if you wanted to demonize a potential invasion target before making your ultimate move, a name like that would make a good start."

At the bottom of the final flight of steps they turned toward the gondola. Stoneheart and Grub were waiting. Grub wore his usual brown robe with a heavy cloak thrown over it for good measure. Stoneheart had his full suit of armor and axe along with a matching fur-lined cloak. Joran wished he had enough magic cloaks for everyone, but when he mentioned it Stoneheart shrugged and pointed out that dwarves were used to the cold.

That didn't make it pleasant for them, but Joran hadn't said anything more on the subject.

The dragon ship leveled out and the captain's voice came through the speaking tubes. "We're in position. Prepare to lower the gondola."

Joran slung his enchanted cloak over his shoulders and Mia

followed his example. The four of them loaded up into the open-air gondola. As soon as they were aboard, it rocked free of the holding clamps and the crew lowered them.

As they descended, Joran took a moment to study the fort. It looked about like Fort Adana only on a smaller scale. In fact, everything was smaller. The courtyard, the main keep, and all the outbuildings were about half the size and the repair hangar was missing altogether. Soldiers manned the walls and towers, so at least he didn't need to worry about running into an army of bile zombies.

A gust of wind rocked the gondola and sent a chill up Joran's spine despite the cloak's magic. Why couldn't all this mess have happened in the summer? Looking for a sleeping dragon was bad enough without having to freeze at the same time.

The gondola settled on the ground with a *thunk* and a soldier wrapped head to toe in a heavy crimson and gold cloak hastened to open the door for them. "Lord Den Cade? Commander Ramirus is waiting for you inside."

"Smart of him," Joran said. "Lead on."

The soldier slammed the gondola door and hurried back toward the keep. They fell in behind him; no one wanting to linger outside longer than they had to. The dragon ship had already begun pulling up the gondola. The plan was for the ship to withdraw to the nearest fort capable of holding it to await word for pickup. No timeline was given and the captain made it clear that he had no intention of returning to Tiber without Joran before summer. If he hadn't returned in five months, even the Iron Princess would understand he wasn't going to.

That seemed fair enough to Joran, so he offered no complaint. In fact, he very much hoped to be done in a month, six weeks at the most. Of course, what he hoped for and what reality might slap him with were often two different things.

Just inside the keep stood a man wearing an imperial dress uniform complete with a golden imperial eagle badge on the chest of his crimson tunic. He stood half a head taller than Joran; probably outweighed him by forty pounds, all of it muscle; and his chiseled face had a perfectly trimmed goatee covering the chin. He reminded Joran a little of Ventor, but he wouldn't hold that against him. All in all, Ramirus looked more like one of the officers you'd find in Tiber not at a border fort.

He offered a smart salute, bringing his fist to his heart. "Welcome, Lord Den Cade, Lady Den Cade. It's a great honor to host you at my modest command."

"Thank you, Commander." Joran couldn't decide if Ramirus was nervous or naturally formal. Either way, as long as he could tell Joran about the area, his personality was irrelevant. "Is there somewhere we can talk? I want to get the details sorted out as soon as possible so we'll be ready to set out at first light."

"Absolutely. My office, crude though it might be, does have chairs enough for all of us. That is, for you and your sister. Your other companions…" Ramirus trailed off as though not entirely certain of Stoneheart and Grub's status.

"My other companions need to know everything I need to know and I'd prefer not to have to repeat it to them. Centurion Stoneheart is an expert in mountain survival and Grub is my personal advisor. I trust you'll treat them with the respect their positions deserve."

Ramirus licked his lips and gave an eager nod. "Of course, my lord. I meant no disrespect to you or your esteemed associates. It's just that we've never had dwarven visitors. I've never even met a dwarf before today. It's come as a surprise. You understand?"

The last sentence came out almost pleading.

Joran understood alright. Ramirus no doubt came from a noble family and immediately dismissed Stoneheart and Grub. They were provincials as well as nonhumans, a combination that, for most of the nobility, reduced their status to somewhere above slaves and below human provincials. The stupidity of that attitude had always bothered Joran, but this was hardly the time to correct a wayward noble.

"I understand that you'll need to find two more chairs, rapidly."

Ramirus looked past Joran at the soldier that stood a pace behind them waiting to be dismissed. "You heard his lordship, two more chairs, right now."

The legionnaire scurried away. Having visited a couple of these forts, Joran wondered if there were two more chairs to be found. Usually the soldiers sat on benches in the mess hall. He hadn't visited the barracks, but doubted that they had much in the way of furniture.

"Shall we head to your office while we wait?" Joran asked.

"Of course, my lord, this way." Ramirus led them toward the rear of the keep.

Only a few strides brought them to a closed door beyond which waited an office. The only reason Joran knew it was an office was the standard desk with a chair behind it with two others facing the first. There were no books or even shelves. Not that there was room for them.

The commander seemed reluctant to sit while Joran stood so he settled in the right-hand chair while Mia moved to stand behind him.

He grinned and glanced at Grub. "Take a seat."

When the dwarf had gotten comfortable, Ramirus gingerly sat in his own chair.

"You may begin your report," Joran said.

"Yes, my lord. The thing is, other than the fact of your arrival, the message gave me no details about your mission."

"We're headed into the mountains to explore the site of a volcanic eruption perhaps seven hundred years ago. We fear enemies of the empire might find powerful magic there to use against us. My task is to confirm what's there and whether a legion will be needed to guard it. It lies approximately one hundred miles into the Land of the Blood Drinkers. I need to know anything you can tell us about the locals and any dangers we're likely to encounter in the mountains."

As he listened, Ramirus's expression grew bleaker by the word. Whatever he'd expected to hear, this wasn't it.

"Problem, Commander?" Mia asked.

"No... Well, sort of. The thing is, I know nothing about the people across the border. I've never seen them and they've never approached, much less attacked the fort. As to the mountains, we don't patrol that deep into them. I've seen goats, and great, soaring eagles of some sort, but that's it. What you'll find further in, I can't say."

So much for local intelligence. Joran scrubbed a hand across his face.

Looked like they'd have to figure it out as they went.

CHAPTER 14

Khashair smiled as his troops lined up in front of the ruined tower, ready and eager for battle. Each of the cultists now stood a good six inches taller. Muscles bulged under their armor and their eyes...

His smile widened. Their eyes now stared straight ahead, as cold and devoid of emotion as a veteran assassin's. Those eyes belonged to creatures who would cut down a fleeing mother before running her baby through. They were ready.

Behind them waited half of his black iron golems. Invulnerable, unstoppable, and unfeeling, they would crush anything that stood between Khashair and victory. The rest would remain behind with his automaton and protect the tower, or more specifically the storeroom beneath it. Not that he imagined anyone breaking through the scrying wards to even find the place.

If you're going to attack, let's go already. My revenge has waited long enough.

"I'm savoring the moment." Golems and men both shifted to look at him when he spoke, clearly expecting an order. "Fine, enough savoring. I already marked a spot not terribly far from the palace for us to appear."

Khashair drew power from the bile pipes running under the tower and opened a portal to Tiber. "Forward. Kill anyone you encounter."

They marched through without hesitation this time. Whatever they'd been before had been washed away and replaced with power and certainty. Far better attributes for warriors.

Bringing up the rear, Gomo paused beside him. "There are a lot of soldiers in Tiber. You sure this is a good idea?"

"Mortal men and second-rate alchemists. Nothing that can stand against them and our magic. Surely you don't fear them."

"Hardly. Then again, I can teleport away if things go badly." The demon shrugged, setting his quills to quivering.

"Your boundless loyalty fills me with joy. Come on."

Gomo strode through and Khashair followed.

On the other side they ended up exactly where he wanted them, in the clearing where the flying ships landed. Only one hovered nearby, though it had a huge golden eagle on the side of the balloon that held it aloft. Must be the emperor's personal transport.

Khashair grinned and pointed at the balloon. A streak of black flames shot from his finger and lanced through the balloon.

A moment later an explosion forced him back a step.

That had been a more energetic response than he expected. He glanced around in time to watch some of his soldiers picking themselves off the ground seeming no worse for wear. As he expected, the potion had increased their durability as well as their strength.

Shouts from the palace drew his gaze away from the flaming wreck that used to be a flying ship.

Hundreds of soldiers were rushing their way from the palace.

Time to see what his new warriors could do.

"Form up! Kill all of them."

The cultists hurried to make a double line fifty people long. They drew their black iron swords and set themselves.

To someone with no idea what they could do, they certainly looked woefully inadequate given the numbers coming against them.

A hundred yards from the field, the soldiers approaching slowed and formed their own ranks. The legionnaires locked their shields in front and the row behind raised their spears to stab over them.

"Golems, charge! Break their formation!" Khashair pointed at the neat square and his black iron golems marched forward, gathering speed as they went.

The imperial soldiers braced themselves for impact as if it would make any difference. No one tried to break and run at least. That showed courage if not brains.

"Want me to lob a few fireballs in?" Gomo asked.

"Not yet. This is their first challenge. I want to see how the enhanced cultists handle it. You'll have a chance to burn plenty of humans later."

Gomo shrugged as if utterly indifferent. Which, to be fair, he probably was. Demons lived on a scale humans, even wizards like Khashair, could hardly fathom. The lives of the humans before Gomo amounted to no more than a blink to him.

The first golem struck the shield wall, helping Khashair refocus.

The construct hit like a battering ram.

Its fellows slammed home a moment later.

The enemy formation shattered like a window meeting a brick.

The golems had barely cleared the final row when the cultists hit the shaken soldiers.

Black iron swords hacked and slashed with little skill but much success.

Each blow killed or maimed its target.

Shields and armor barely slowed them and soon the field was silent save for the crackling flames.

"I'd call that a successful test." Khashair smiled. He might lack the numbers to rule the empire, but he certainly had enough to destroy it.

Alexandra hated attending the weekly God's Day sermon. It was one of the main reasons she preferred being out of the city as much as possible. She pitied Marcus having to come every week, but he didn't seem to mind and his wife was as devout a woman as you'd hope to meet. If word ever got out that The One God was a fantasy, she'd be the most heartbroken.

Well, after the pope at least.

Even Father only came to church on the four high holy days. Not that anyone dared claim he was insufficiently pious. As long as one person from the imperial family attended, that seemed to be enough to satisfy everyone.

Today the pews were packed from front to back with the rich and powerful, all dressed to the nines and not looking at all humble. Not that the imperial nobility were known for their humility, but you'd think at least one day a week they might leave a pound or two of gold at home.

Sunlight shone through the stained-glass windows, sending colorful designs dancing around the church. Some of the younger kids stared at them with wide eyes.

Ah, to be young again. No responsibilities, no idea how dangerous the world was, just wide-eyed innocence.

She glanced around and spotted Joran's family two rows behind her. Jorik looked about as comfortable as she felt, but

Sestia wore a bright smile, seeming fully in her element. The sermon would start soon, so she didn't take time to go talk to them. Maybe later, assuming they were still around after she spoke to Rufious.

Unless the church had better news than she did, the conversation would be short. Nothing of note had reached her ears since he visited the palace. She did get confirmation that Joran had reached the border without issue, but that didn't concern the church. It pleased her to know he'd made it to his destination without getting knocked out of the air this time. Of course, knowing why he was there did nothing to soothe her nerves.

This might well be the most dangerous task he'd undertaken to date.

Her thoughts were cut off when one of the doors opened and Septimus emerged in full regalia. His white robe and silly hat both seemed to glow in the sunlight. Joran probably could have told her exactly how that trick worked.

She swallowed a sigh, wishing once again that he hadn't left.

Behind the pope, still standing in the shadow of the doorway, stood Rufious. When she caught his eye, he offered a faint nod. Looked like the conference was still on.

Septimus raised his hands and everyone sat.

Now she just had to make it through the bloviating without falling asleep or drawing the dagger hidden high on her thigh under her fancy robe. Stabbing the pope would end the sermon quickly, but not in the way she wanted.

And so he droned on about morality and doing the right thing. Or something like that. Alexandra didn't really pay attention. Despite her lack of interest, she did manage to make the circle over her heart and say, "So say we all" in time with the rest of the faithful.

As soon as she did, youths in white tunics paraded out from another door, each carrying a golden plate. One of them came to Alexandra first and she dutifully dropped five gold imperials into the plate. Not overly generous, but if anyone had a complaint, they saw fit not to share it with her. Considering the church kidnapped her soon-to-be husband not that long ago, she figured that was more than enough.

As the kids worked their way toward the back of the church, Septimus and Rufious came down from the altar and shook hands with their flock. When Rufious grasped her hand, he leaned in and whispered, "Nothing."

"Us either," she whispered back.

And so ended the secret meeting.

She took a single stride toward the exit before an explosion rocked the church. It sounded distant, but still powerful enough to shake the supports.

Her first thought was an accident with alchemist's fire, but she quickly dismissed the thought. No amateurs would have access and properly trained alchemists would never make such a mistake. So either they'd been betrayed again, or the explosion was something else.

She didn't have time to puzzle it out before another blast, smaller, but still powerful, shook the building.

That one sounded closer.

"What's going on?" shouted someone from the back of the church.

The question opened a deluge of shouts and demands for information. As if the people that had been sitting beside them for the last hour knew any more about what was happening than they did.

"Stay calm, everyone," Septimus said in a more soothing voice than she would have believed him capable of. "White Knights will be sent to investigate. You should remain here until we know what's going on."

Probably didn't want any of his patrons getting killed. The dead tended to be a good deal less generous than the living.

She gave a little shake of her head. That was a low thought even for her.

Alexandra caught Rufious's eye and nodded off to the side. When they put some distance between themselves and the rest of the flock she said, "I need to get out there and see what's going on. I know there's got to be another way out of the church."

"Are you sure that's wise? The Iron Guards are out front. Better if you go that way."

She shook her head. "If, The One God forbid, this is some sort of attack, I'll certainly be a target. Anyone looking for me, will look for the guards first. I have a better chance of sneaking back to the palace on my own. Though if you'd be so kind as to send someone to let the guards know I've gone, that would be helpful."

Rufious made a face. "Do you think that's likely? How would someone get into Third Circle without having to fight their way through First and Second? That's the whole point of having the circles, isn't it?"

Alexandra hadn't told them about the magic circle Joran found in the slums. Another explosion in the distance made it clear that this wasn't the time to do so either. "It's a long story, and when things calm down I'll be sure to tell it to you, but suffice it to say there is a way of getting into Third Circle, a magical way. The problem is we have no idea how to stop it, research on the mysteries of magic having been banned by the church."

"It seemed like a good idea at the time. Follow me. I'll show you the back door."

Rufious started toward the door where he'd stood watching the sermon and she hurried to follow. They wound their way through gray, undecorated halls for far longer than she would have thought necessary to reach the back of the church.

At last, Rufious stopped in front of an unmarked door and

pushed it open. It looked out on a small grassy area. She slipped out and turned toward the palace. A cloud of black smoke rose from the landing field.

Again she considered and dismissed an accident. Father had no trips planned, which meant no one would be loading anything on his ship, including a bomb. No, someone had to have snuck in using magic.

Whoever it was must be an idiot. And the First and Second legions would make that clear to them. But first she had to get over there and get the defense organized. The question was how best to do it without drawing the attention of the attackers.

Another explosion was followed by a rising pillar of smoke. This one closer to the palace.

What the hell were those morons doing? No way should any enemy force smaller than a legion be forcing its way closer to the palace, even with magic.

She shook her head and ran toward the rear of the palace. Making a loop wide enough to avoid the attackers would cost her time, but on her own—hell, even with her guards—there was no way she'd be able to deal with an enemy strong enough to push the First and Second back.

Alexandra paused at the border between the church and palace grounds. This was as close as she dared get to the landing field. Even from a distance she could see Father's personal dragon ship had been reduced to flaming rubble. The last few months had certainly been rough on dragon ships. They were down to two operational ships and neither of them were close.

Of course, for a powerful wizard, the dragon ships were little more than big targets. Better by far if they stayed on the ground and out of sight.

Her gaze shifted to the force of black-clad attackers even now hacking their way through the Second Legion. She squinted. If there were over two hundred enemies she'd resign as supreme commander.

Two hundred shouldn't last ten minutes against a legion, much less two.

Another figure in black, this one unarmed, pointed at a century of approaching reinforcements and a ball of black flames shot out.

It exploded, sending men flying in all directions.

That certainly explained some of their problem. Beside the wizard, a red-skinned dwarf loosed bloodred flames into the flank of the Second, collapsing their defense and allowing the attackers to push even further forward.

Where were the bloody alchemists? Maybe a little fire of their own would give the enemy pause.

She shook her head. Enough screwing around. Time to find Father and Marcus and put some distance between them and the wizard.

How she'd manage that particular miracle was another matter altogether.

———

Emperor Marcus Tiberius glared around at the imperial guards standing between him and the massively heavy door to his suite. Even more men were standing outside in front of it. As soon as the first explosion sounded, his personal guards had hustled him to safety. Two more units were out fetching his son and his family. Alexandra was at the church and hopefully safe, at least for the moment.

He nearly smiled. No, Alexandra would no doubt already be on her way here to try and stop whoever had the audacity to attack his capital city. He hoped she succeeded. Given the few spotty reports he'd gotten, it sounded like nothing the legions had tried did anything to stop the invaders.

The facts that they were led by a wizard and a wizard had been the one to attack the church's fortress seemed more than a coincidence. Perhaps the stolen artifact lent the invaders their overwhelming power.

So many questions and so few answers.

Another explosion sounded, too close for comfort this time. At this rate, the enemy would be inside the palace before long.

"What's going on out there?" he demanded of no one in particular.

"The last messenger hasn't returned yet, Your Imperial Majesty," the unit commander said. "No word on the crown prince either."

Marcus wanted to rant and rave, but it would do more harm than good. He wanted the guards focused on the problem, not their petulant ruler. Not that any of them would dare call him petulant to his face. Or behind his back, for that matter. If word of such disrespect reached him, he'd be forced to have the person responsible executed and he really didn't want to have to do that. Especially to men that had dedicated their lives to protecting his.

A heavy blow sounded on the suite door.

All fifty guards lowered their spears.

"The crown prince and his family have arrived," one of the guards outside said.

Finally. "Open the door!"

The guards hastened to obey though they made sure to open it only enough to allow Marcus, Octavia, and the boys to slip through. All of them wore comfortable, informal robes, and judging by Marcus's hair, he'd been roused from his bed.

"What in the world is going on, Father?" Marcus asked.

The emperor glanced at his grandsons. The boys were only four and six. They didn't need to hear this. No doubt being hustled out of their suite by the guards had shaken them enough. At least they weren't crying, for which he was grateful.

"Octavia," Marcus said. When she looked at him, he gave a little nod toward the far corner of the suite.

"Come on, boys," she said. "Let's play over here."

She took each of them by the hand and led them out of earshot.

"The palace is under attack by magic users and a force of soldiers," the emperor said. "The last report we got made it sound like the First and Second had no hope of keeping them out of the palace, but they were still fighting hard."

"Then why do we linger?" Marcus asked. "We should escape while we can."

The emperor shook his head. "We have to wait until they enter the palace. Once they're all inside, we can slip out and avoid notice. Their numbers aren't so great that they can attack inside and seal the exterior. It's a risk, but one we need to take."

"I don't like it," Marcus said.

"Nor do I, but it's our best hope of escaping. Where we'll escape to is another matter. Anyone strong enough to attack us here, could attack us anywhere."

An alarming thought if ever there was one.

CHAPTER 15

It took Alexandra far too long to make it around the palace grounds to the rear wall. There really should've been some guards around, but they'd probably all diverted either to the battle out front or gone inside to prepare for room-to-room fighting. It wasn't something they trained for regularly, but every palace guard studied the basics of fighting in the palace.

Hopefully they'd taken the training seriously.

At least the attackers lacked the numbers to send anyone on a flanking maneuver. So far anyway.

Now, to get inside and find her family.

Alexandra ran her hand along the smooth, gray stone. The entrance was around here somewhere. She remembered when Father showed her how to open it years ago. He'd laughed at the time and said she'd never need to use it, but better safe than sorry. How she wished he'd been right.

A stone shifted under her hand and a section of wall slid inward. She slipped inside, found the first alcove, and pulled out a light vial. A few hard shakes got it going. Now that she could see, Alexandra closed the hidden door.

Cobwebs hung from the ceiling and walls in a thick veil. Dust filled the air, tickling her nose. It wasn't like the servants could come in here and clean, but surely there had to be some kind of alchemy thing to keep the vermin out. She made a mental note to ask Joran when he got back. As far as she knew, he was the only alchemist that knew about the passages and he might well be the only one that had ever been told they existed.

Alexandra hitched her skirt up enough to pull her dagger before setting out. She didn't expect to run into the enemy, but a really big spider seemed well within the realm of possibility. A shiver ran down her spine. In Stello Province she'd seen some of the spiders that called the jungle home. Hopefully none of them hitched a ride back on a dragon ship.

Ten strides in and her hair was covered in filth. The ever-louder explosions outside helped to distract her. The only thing that mattered was getting everyone to safety. She could take a bath if they survived.

At the first intersection she paused to check the subtle signs engraved in the stone. No one outside the family would know what they meant, but for Alexandra, they served as a map.

She turned left and kept moving. Everyone would be gathered in Father's suite. That was standard protocol if the palace was attacked. Not that anyone had ever remotely expected to have to follow that particular protocol.

A loud sigh slipped past her lips. It seemed lately they'd been doing a lot of things they never expected would be necessary.

If the current crisis ended with the empire intact and the Tiberius family still ruling it, they would have to make some serious decisions about their future and not just in regard to security. Everything needed to change, especially their attitude toward magic. The empire needed wizards of their own and Alexandra would see that they got them even if she had to personally beat reality into every churchman.

Halfway to Father's suite she paused to peek out one of the

peepholes. No servants or guards running frantically through the halls. That was a good sign. It meant the guards were in place and ready for room-to-room fighting. The servants should have evacuated to the basement. They were all nobodies, which, hopefully, meant none of the attackers would be eager to kill them.

She moved on, hurrying to reach her family before they decided to make a break for it.

Five minutes brought her to the door to Father's suite. There were no peepholes here, so she rapped a careful rhythm on the door with the hilt of her dagger. Marcus and Father would recognize it.

Faint footsteps were followed by Marcus tapping his code on the other side. She let out a breath. He'd made it safe and sound.

Alexandra opened the door and they shared a hug. Father was there a moment later to collect one of his own.

"Despite the risk, I knew you'd come," Father said.

"Of course. My original plan was to take command of the defenses, but when I saw the enemy's magic it became clear that our only option is to flee. I assume the only reason you're still here is that they haven't breached the door yet."

Father nodded. "It won't be long. The problem is, I have no idea where we need to go. Where will be safe?"

"Nowhere, but for now I suggest we take the long tunnel then head east. The Fourth is still intact and at full strength. With a little luck, we might even be able to signal the dragon ship we sent to investigate the church fortress. I'd feel a lot better with a few dozen extra alchemists backing us up. Not that the ones on duty seem to be doing much good at the moment. Even the White Knights might be useful."

"You saw the enemy?" Marcus asked.

"From a distance. I estimate their number at under two hundred, but there are two wizards. Or maybe one wizard and a creature of some sort. It looked like a dwarf, but I've never seen a dwarf with red skin like that. Anyway, both of them hurled fireballs one after the other, blasting our formations to bits before the soldiers could hit them. Every fighter had black armor and weapons. I fear their gear is made of the same stuff as the sword the demon wanted."

"The One God be merciful," Father muttered, not seeming to realize he'd spoken out loud.

If such a being had existed, Alexandra certainly wouldn't have turned his mercy down. But at the moment they were going to have to trust themselves.

"Once they breach the door," Alexandra said. "You need to order the guards outside to join the general defense while we take the ones in here with us."

"Why?" Marcus asked.

"Because the ones inside have seen the secret door," Father answered for her. "If they get captured, the wizard might pull that information out of their minds. And the ones outside need to leave so they don't draw attention to my suite, which might also lead to the discovery of the passages. Good thinking, sweetheart."

A thud on the door ended the conversation. The unit commander strode over and opened it a foot or so. "The enemy has breached the palace."

And that was it. For hundreds of years no enemy force had entered Tiber, much less the imperial palace. And now it had fallen into enemy hands in hours. If she wasn't living it, Alexandra would have sworn such a thing was impossible. Of course, her range of possibilities had expanded a fair bit over the last year.

"Give the order, Unit Commander," Father said.

The commander bowed and stuck his head out into the hall. When the door closed again, the sound of heavy boots marching away reached them.

"Time for us to go as well," Alexandra said. "I'll take point."

"You most certainly will not," Father said. "The imperial guardsmen will take the lead."

"I appreciate your concern, Father, but we can't take the time to stop every time we reach an intersection. I can read the symbols and am the most expendable of the three of us." His face twisted up, but they both knew she was telling the simple truth. "I'm not going to do anything crazy."

Marcus approached with little Vel on his back piggyback style while Octavia held Marcus the Twenty-Eighth's hand. It was time to go.

"Unit Commander!" Father said.

The man trotted up. "Your Imperial Majesty?"

"You will follow directly behind my daughter. You will keep her safe. If anything happens to her, it had better be over your dead body. Understood?"

He clapped his fist to his heart. "Perfectly, sire."

They set out, Alexandra in the lead, the unit commander behind her followed by twenty of his men, then the rest of the imperial family was followed by the remaining thirty. The soldiers in their heavy armor made more noise than she would have preferred, but the stone walls and explosions should keep the enemy from hearing them.

At least, that's what she kept telling herself.

Minutes passed punctuated by the occasional muffled explosion. A few times the walls shook and once Vel started to whimper. Fortunately Marcus soothed the boy before full-blown sobs had a chance to break out. Despite the situation, she smiled. Her brother had turned out to be a good father. That pleased her a great deal.

At last they reached the entrance to the long tunnel. Alexandra didn't remember which of her ancestors had ordered the passage dug, but today she was very happy for the paranoia of the nobility.

A heavy door blocked the passage. She didn't even try to open it, instead moving aside to let the unit commander grasp the heavy iron ring attached to the door. His shoulder bunched and with a grunt of effort the foot-thick imperial steel door swung open.

"Where does it lead?" Octavia asked.

"Well beyond the city and hopefully to at least temporary safety." Alexandra motioned the lead guards to go through first.

She'd done her part to get them here. The long tunnel didn't branch, so they couldn't get lost.

When he left, she feared Joran would be the one walking into trouble. How little she had known.

CHAPTER 16

Khashair scowled at the empty corridor in front of him. The remnants of the broken legions had fled and he let them go. Sending his limited forces to chase them down was just asking for trouble. Besides, the ones he actually wanted to kill were inside, not among the rabble running as far and fast as their legs would carry them.

Speaking of rabble, where were the interior guards? Surely they didn't intend to simply let him go on his way without resisting. Reaching out with his magic he sensed many life forces, but they were all over the place. If someone was coming to kill him, Khashair would have ordered all his guards to cluster around him. There was a large gathering in the basement. Could that be the emperor?

Hurry up. The longer we delay, the better the chances of the pope escaping. It's his fault she died and he must pay for it!

"So you've told me more than once. The imperial family is more important, but rest assured the pope and his lackeys will suffer the same fate soon enough." He turned his attention to the cultists behind him. "Spread out, kill anyone that resists, and find the imperial family."

The group broke up, some going left, others right, and the rest straight ahead. It shouldn't take them long to flush the targets out. No doubt some brave guards would do their best to save the royals, but all they would do was die in vain. No ordinary men had a chance against his enhanced soldiers.

"Are you sure it's wise to send them hunting on their own?" Gomo asked. "Most of your soldiers were bandits at best and farmers at worst before taking up their new career."

"It's necessary. They need to learn how to fight and carry out my orders on their own. I won't be there every second to hold their hands. This is a good chance to see who has what it takes and who doesn't."

Gomo shrugged and said no more about it.

Not that the demon didn't have a point. If the cultists came through this unscathed it would be a miracle. Even weaklings got lucky once in a while.

Minutes ticked by as the number of life forces slowly dwindled. Khashair assumed that if the imperial family had been slain, someone would have hurried to tell him. In this case, no news likely meant bad news.

About halfway through the extermination, a burst of powerful magic drew his attention. It came from the far end of the palace. No one here was strong enough to create such an effect. In fact, he could think of only one person that he had encountered capable of such magic. Surely she wouldn't be stupid enough to try to take him on again, much less in the daylight.

"Did you sense that?" Gomo asked as if it were possible for him to miss such a powerful spell.

"Yes. The true archbishop, do you think?"

"I can't imagine the vampire would be stupid enough to come here in the middle of the day. Even inside the palace she would be badly reduced in power. No, I suspect this is something else. Probably something she sent in hopes that it would either kill or weaken you."

Khashair snorted. "If she imagines there's anything she can do to hurt me, then she's an idiot."

Don't underestimate her. The archbishop has been around for a long time. She may know some tricks that you don't.

If she didn't know his deepest secret, the secret of how to draw on the power of Black Bile from a distance, then nothing else she knew would matter.

Khashair winced when one of his soldiers died. Part of the magic that created them also let him know their status. While not perfect, it did make clear when one of them died.

Another fell a second later.

Clearly whatever had appeared was beyond the abilities of his servants to defeat.

"Come along," Khashair said. "Let's go see what kind of playmate she sent us."

In the time it took to reach the far end of the palace, three more of his servants had died. Five dead in less than two minutes. That seemed impossible given their weapons, armor, and physical enhancements. Perhaps he *had* underestimated her.

They rounded a corner in time to see a cultist get cut in half by a partially melted man wielding a black iron sword.

Khashair drew power from the pipes running under the palace.

He had no chance to loose his spell before the creature sprinted away out of sight.

A snarl twisted his lips. That had to be the last overseer. But it felt stronger than the one he killed to the south.

"That was a Hell-forged blade," Gomo said.

Khashair snapped a look at him. "You're sure?"

"I should be, I made enough of them. In the hands of a demon, even a weak one bound to a corpse, it's no wonder your soldiers are having trouble."

As if to punctuate Gomo's pronouncement, another cultist died.

"I'll deal with it myself. You find the imperial family." When Gomo nodded, Khashair sent the power he'd gathered into his body and sprinted away at near-blinding speed.

It didn't take long for him to catch up to the overseer. He rounded a corner just in time to watch another of his cultists get cut in half like his black armor was tissue paper.

He hated to admit it, but Hell-forged blades were vastly superior to the copies they made in the empire.

The overseer glared at him with glowing red eyes and charged.

Shocked that the creature would dare fight him directly nearly proved Khashair's undoing.

Lucky for him, his enhanced speed allowed him to leap back ahead of a powerful chop that would have split him in half.

Before the overseer had a chance to recover, he drew more power and blasted it with the unmaking spell.

It actually resisted for a few seconds before exploding in a burst of flesh and bile.

An instant later a rune on the sword flashed and it vanished.

So much for expanding his arsenal. But at least the creature wouldn't kill any more of his servants.

From a safe distance away, some of the survivors were staring at him. They didn't look shaken exactly, the potion they drank wouldn't allow that emotion, but the overseer's appearance and his fight with it certainly affected them somehow.

It struck him a moment later. Khashair was supposed to be the archbishop and the overseers served him. Seeing him fight one undercut that lie. Not enough for them to break the spell that made them completely loyal, but it certainly didn't help.

"It's alright," he said. "The imposter seized control of the overseer and forced it to attack. It's a waste, but destroying it was necessary. Back to the hunt."

They bowed and hurried back the way they'd come. How much of his lie had they believed? Probably not much, but in the end, he didn't really care as long as they continued to obey.

Now to see if Gomo had any better luck finding the imperial family than his mortal servants.

———

"Miserable, disagreeable wizards," Gomo grumbled as he stalked down the hall. How the hell was he supposed to find the imperial family? They might be anywhere.

The vampire had been bad enough, but there was no one more arrogant than an overmage. The human, assuming he still qualified as a human, said to find the imperial family. Sounded simple enough until you remembered that Gomo was a forgeling. His skills ran toward making things and burning things. Divination wasn't his forte.

Still, if he didn't at least try and find them, Khashair was apt to put a binding on him and that didn't suit Gomo at all. He preferred to at least have the option to run should worst come to worst. In fact, he seriously considered just vanishing and trying his luck elsewhere. Only his fear that the vengeful human might hunt him down and do something even worse as punishment kept him wandering the halls in the vain hope that he might stumble across the right human.

Not that he even knew what they looked like. Killing the ones in the fanciest outfits might be safe enough.

Gomo scratched his quills. From the surging power behind him, it felt like Khashair would be done soon. And he hadn't even found a single human. His master wouldn't be best pleased by that.

There was a burst of ether and Gomo found himself nose to nose with a kid in a brown robe. He had just enough time to wonder how a twelve-year-old could teleport before a blast of lightning crashed into his chest, wrapped around his heart, and started to squeeze.

"I'm really sorry about this," the kid said. "But the archbishop says leaving a demon on the field is a bad idea. Personally, I wanted to capture you and bring you back to fight my pets. They've never fought a demon before."

Gomo tried to say something but only a gurgling moan escaped his lips.

"The other guy's coming back, so I need to wrap things up. So long."

Gomo retained consciousness just long enough to feel his heart explode. An instant later his essence was absorbed back into Abaddon's hell.

When Beastmaster appeared in his scrying chamber he found Fane leaning against the tripod that held his crystal ball, a big fang-filled smile on her face. He found that almost as unsettling as her fang-filled snarls. At least a happy Fane usually meant less work for him.

"I blasted the demon like you said."

"You had no trouble?"

Beastmaster raised an eyebrow. "It was just a forgeling. I still think you should've let me capture him to train my pets. He was so weak, I could've bound him in five minutes."

"You didn't have five minutes. Khashair arrived only a second after you escaped. That wouldn't have been a fight you wanted."

"True. Did you see what you wanted to?"

"I did. I saw the spell that lets him draw the bile's power up through the pipes. It also looks like he can't reach the deeper lakes."

"So you can copy it?" Beastmaster plopped down on the hard

stone floor. He was getting hungry and, unlike Fane, he needed a nap.

"I should be able to." Fane moved away from the crystal ball and started pacing. "The problem is, it'll take me weeks if not months or years to master it to the degree he has. And if I'm not faster than him activating his own spell, well, you know what happens then."

"Boom."

"Exactly. No, I think our move is to cut him off from his power source. I read that book you brought back and unless I'm mistaken, there's a master cutoff that shuts down all the pipes and drains them back into the lakes. That would certainly be easier than closing all the valves manually."

Beastmaster frowned and rubbed his eyes. "Why would the overmages build such a weakness into their system?"

"My guess? For when repairs were needed, or the network needed to be extended into their next province. Whatever the reason, the shutoff isn't far from the castle where we found Khashair."

She stared at Beastmaster who groaned. "And you want me to go turn it off."

"Indeed. Unlike me, you can operate during the day without issue. If you run into something too powerful for you, contact me after sunset and I can back you up. Until the pipe network is shut down, we have no hope of winning. Do you disagree?"

Beastmaster shook his head. Whether he disagreed or not was irrelevant. She would still expect him to do what she said.

"I need to eat and sleep for a few hours before I leave. You fed the prisoner, right?"

"Yes. If this plan doesn't work, I have another, but it's a much longer shot."

Beastmaster almost laughed. If her backup was a longer shot than shutting down an ancient network of black iron pipes whose function they didn't fully understand using a mechanism neither of them had ever seen, then the odds of success hardly bore thinking about.

———

K hashair had barely taken a step toward where he sensed the demon when another powerful burst of magic drew his attention. It hadn't been quite as strong as the one that heralded the overseer's arrival, but it had been plenty strong. And far too close to Gomo for comfort. While he had no particular fondness for or loyalty to the demon, he was a useful servant and powerful addition to Khashair's little army. If anything happened to him, it would be inconvenient.

He rushed away at high speed, the walls a blur on either side of him.

Ten strides from Gomo's location he sensed another burst of magic then nothing.

He closed the distances and found a rapidly dissolving puddle of sludge that used to be Gomo. Whoever teleported in was far stronger than the overseer. Another of the vampire's allies no doubt.

She'd pay for this. Whatever else he might have been, Gomo had belonged to him and no one stole from Khashair.

When this raid was over, he'd make a concerted effort to track her down and end the threat once and for all.

After the church.

"Yes, after the cursed church. I'll burn the wretched place to the ground with every priest I can find inside if it will free me from your endless complaints."

It took half an hour, but finally one of the cultists tiptoed toward him. Had he drawn the short straw?

Khashair smiled. He wasn't apt to waste a perfectly good servant just because he delivered some bad news. "Speak."

"We searched the entire palace, Archbishop, but found no

sign of the imperial family. We killed all the guards and located the servants in the basement. They offered no resistance and per your order we left them alone. Do you have further orders?"

Continuing the search probably wouldn't help. The emperor doubtless had some secret way to escape on the off chance the palace was attacked. Khashair certainly did when he ruled his territory. Though his was magical rather than mundane. The ones he really wanted were almost certainly far away and since he had no idea what they looked like, he couldn't scry for them.

"We march on the church. Perhaps we'll find the pope less well prepared."

Don't count on it. Septimus might be a pig and a liar, but he's smart enough to know when to run. All this noise and wasted time will have sent him into the deepest, darkest hole he can find.

"Perhaps, but we can still burn the church down and kill any priests we find." Khashair turned toward the exit. "Let's go!"

They emerged from the palace but found no soldiers waiting to resume the fight. It seemed they could learn if given a sufficiently clear lesson. On the landing field, the dragon ship still burned away, great clouds of black smoke rising into the clear air. So far, destroying it was the only truly useful thing he'd done. And he hardly counted it valuable enough to make up for the demon's loss.

The church waited just the other side of the palace grounds. Khashair marched at the head of his little force, an invisible shield in place should anyone take a shot at him. Not that he'd seen any archers, but in enemy territory, precautions had to be taken.

No one tried to stop them and soon enough they reached the foot of the stairs leading up to the church doors. Inside they found the pews empty and a single priest waiting near the altar. The young man couldn't have been more than twenty.

"Welcome, everyone, to the First Church of The One God. I'm afraid you missed the sermon, but if you wish to pray, you're free to do so." The priest's voice quavered a little, but overall he seemed calm enough considering nearly a hundred armed men had barged into the church.

"I'd like to have a word with the pope," Khashair said.

"My apologies, sir, but His Holiness had to leave on important business. I'm the only one here, but if you tell me the problem, I'll do my best to help."

Khashair wanted to kill him just so he wouldn't have to listen to his pious stupidity any longer. A simple spell confirmed that the church was indeed empty save the obviously expendable fellow speaking to them.

"When will the pope return?" Khashair asked.

"No one tells me things like that, sir. His Eminence, Cardinal Rufious, told me to welcome anyone that came and to tend to things here until they returned. Beyond that, I know nothing."

"That is unfortunate."

Khashair pointed and a blast of lightning blew the man to smithereens.

"Do you wish to burn the church down? I'm perfectly willing to oblige, but I fear we'll find no churchmen to add to the pyre."

A wave of depression washed over Khashair, but he received no other answer.

His hunt, it seemed, had accomplished little beyond showing off his power and proving to his future subjects that they had no hope of ever defeating him.

"I suppose that's enough fun for today. Back to the tower, everyone."

He opened a portal and his soldiers and golems marched through without complaint. Not the start he'd hoped for and the loss of Gomo stung, but all in all he thought he'd made a point. Eventually he would find the emperor and then he'd make another, greater point.

CHAPTER 17

Despite Joran's desire to set out as soon as possible, Stoneheart insisted that they spend two days at the fort getting used to the elevation. Though well below the peaks, the fort was several thousand feet higher than Tiber. Stoneheart assured them that they'd appreciate the time to acclimate when they started climbing.

Since overriding the person he considered an expert on this sort of thing would be beyond stupid, Joran forced himself to relax, or at least to try and relax. Practicing his new magical abilities in the room he shared with Mia, and out of sight of any overly devout soldiers, did wonders for his nerves.

And now their two days were up. Provisioned and ready, they set out for the mountains jutting up in the distance. Joran had made a map based on everything he'd read, but details were sketchy at best and he doubted its accuracy. Stoneheart had tucked it in his belt pouch after saying he spent the last day studying and memorizing what little detail it held.

"Ready, Lord Den Cade?" Stoneheart asked when Joran had finished adjusting his cloak.

Joran glanced at Mia who nodded then at Grub who gave a

nod of his own. "Ready as I'll ever be. Let's get this show on the road."

Stoneheart waved at the soldiers on duty at the gate and they swung the heavy doors open. Unlike a proper fortress, the border fort only had wooden doors with a beam to hold them shut. Stone walls and a portcullis would've been nice, but at the edge of the empire it didn't make sense. In the event of an invasion, a wooden fort would be easier to retake or more likely burn down.

They headed west along a snow-covered dirt path far too rough to be called a road. In fact, it made the rutted coach road to Stello Province look positively smooth in comparison. They needed to travel ten miles or so before turning a little north. Eight of those miles would be through the Land of the Blood Drinkers. There was no indication of settlements this close to the border, but as Ramirus said, they didn't make patrols outside the empire.

"What do you think we'll find?" Mia asked.

"A big hole full of Black Bile, hopefully with a deeply asleep dragon at the bottom. That's my best-case scenario."

"What's your worst-case scenario?" Grub asked from his position at the rear of the column.

"That the dragon wakes up as soon as we get close and kills everyone and everything in the empire."

"Is that likely?" Mia asked.

"I doubt it, but I don't actually know. I don't know what the overmages did to wake it up the first time. I don't think they just showed up. Given what we know, they probably tried to enslave it. We are definitely not going to try that. Just a quick peek to confirm it's there and we're gone. Who knows, maybe it'll even be grateful to have some guards to keep anyone from bothering it."

Grub barked a laugh and Joran had to admit that his scenario was pretty farfetched. Still, if he could think of the potential bad things, why not balance it out with some good?

Once they left the vicinity of the fort, the path entered a stand of tall evergreens. The shadows immediately made it feel ten degrees colder. Joran shivered and imagined all manner of enemies hiding just out of sight.

They marched for hours, seeing nothing more threatening than an annoyed squirrel that barked at them from the branches. An hour after lunch they left the forest and started across an open plain covered with six inches of snow. Stoneheart turned north, toward the mountains.

Joran shaded his eyes. Was there smoke rising from them?

"Is that smoke in the mountains?" he asked.

"I'm not sure. I think the source might be lower," Mia said. "The mountains don't look like the kind of place you'd want to build a village. The dragon, you think?"

Joran shrugged. "Maybe."

"Might be a foundry," Stoneheart said without looking back. "If there's a mine, they could be processing the ore."

Joran smiled to himself. Speculating was a fun way to make the time go by quicker. Not having anyone trying to kill them at the moment was nice as well. It couldn't last of course. Nothing good seemed to lately.

As if the universe was listening, half a mile later the snow crunched and a dozen figures armed with spears stood in a circle all around them.

Mia instantly drew her sword and shifted to protect Joran. Stoneheart had his axe out a second later and Grub was only a fraction slower drawing his shortsword.

After a tense few seconds without bloodshed, Joran took a moment to study the new arrivals. They wore heavy leather pants and shirts made from animal skins with the tails still attached. Their skin was lighter than an imperial's. Some strange designs had been painted on their skin with red paint.

Joran shifted his gaze to the ether but saw no magic around them.

How had they snuck up on them with no cover or camouflage?

Since they couldn't just stand here forever, he said, "Hello. My name is Joran Den Cade. Can you understand me?"

The men stared at him but didn't speak. They also didn't point their spears at him, so that was a good sign. The tricky part would be getting a translation potion out of his kit without them thinking he planned something aggressive.

With exaggerated slowness, Joran took his kit off his shoulder and opened the top.

Still no reaction from the locals.

He took out a vial and downed the contents.

When he felt the magic take hold, he tried again. "Hello."

Their eyes widened and they all started talking far too quickly for him to understand even with the translation effect.

"Please, could you slow down? And maybe just one of you speak at a time?"

They fell silent but now they were frowning. Had he committed some kind of cultural error? No one knew anything about these people, so it wasn't beyond the realm of possibility.

Finally, one of them, the tallest and most muscular, said, "What brings you to our land?"

"We're just passing through. My team and I seek to explore the mountains." Should he take a chance? "There was an eruption long ago and we wish to see the caldera."

"That place is taboo. You will find nothing in the pit save evil."

Certainly sounded like the dragon was still there. "I understand, but enemies of my people seek to wake that evil and unleash it on our home. My job is to confirm what's there and see what can be done to keep anyone else from gaining access. Can you help us?"

All twelve of them started jabbering in a blur of words. Joran didn't even try to listen. How the hell did they understand anything the others were saying?

"What's going on?" Mia asked.

"I'm not sure, but it doesn't look like they want to fight. With any luck we might secure ourselves a guide through the mountains. At the very least it seems they know about the caldera, though they made no mention of the dragon, only that evil lived there."

She whispered, "Do you trust them?"

Keeping his voice equally low he said, "Not especially, but this is a foreign land. We have no power here and if we have to fight our way through The One God only knows how many people, we're doomed to failure before we even begin. Best to try talking first and hopefully get the lay of the land."

At last, the babble died down and the leader or spokesman or whatever he was said, "We will take you to our wiseman. He will be better able to explain the danger. Follow us."

He turned and started toward the smoke Joran spotted earlier. His companions fell in behind him. Everyone finally put their weapons away and they followed along. No more words were spoken on either side and near sunset they arrived at a village of one-room log cabins. The smoke came from many chimneys, and piles of wood stacked nearly to the roofs sat behind each building. One cabin, the largest of the bunch, waited in the middle of the village. Their guides led them to it and one of them knocked.

When the door opened, the oldest man Joran had ever seen stood in the doorway. His face was a mass of wrinkles and his blue eyes were sunk deep into his skull. Not a single hair grew on his face or head. Despite the heat blasting out of the cabin, he wore a heavy fur blanket over his shoulders.

While Joran and his companions waited, a thirteen-way conversation took place. The cacophony gave him a headache.

Though that might have also been from his potion trying to translate so many voices at once.

Their chat was blessedly brief and at last the old man said, "If you seek the Pit of Darkness, I will speak with you. Enter and be welcome."

Joran bowed and led the way in. The heat felt wonderful, but he suspected they'd be sweating in five minutes. There was no furniture in the solitary chamber beyond a few cushions littering the floor near the blazing fireplace.

The old man sat on one of the cushions and motioned for Joran and his companions to join him. When everyone had gotten as comfortable as siting on the floor allowed, Joran said, "Thank you for speaking with us. Though we're neighbors, I know little about your people and culture. I hope I did nothing to offend."

"We are not easily offended. Though you trespassed on our tribe's land, when confronted by our warriors, you showed restraint and did not attack. That is well. I would hear your purpose in your own words."

Joran gave him an edited version of the last six months. "The dragon we fear sleeps in what you call the Pit of Darkness. It is powerful and evil. We hope to keep what happened in the east from happening here."

"All right-thinking beings desire that the beast of darkness stays asleep forever. That your enemy is mad enough to seek to wake it tells me all I need to know. What can I do to help?"

Joran smiled. "Have you been to the pit? If you could confirm the dragon's presence, that would save us a lot of walking."

The old man wheezed a laugh. "No one goes to the pit. Only death and madness live there. I seek neither."

"Is there anything you can tell me about it?"

"I can tell you what our legends say. Bear in mind that they are only legends. The truth is often seen between the lines."

"We would be honored to hear your legends."

The wiseman took a deep breath. "Long ago, it is said that a great beast flew to this land seeking rest. It landed and lay down. To ensure it wouldn't be disturbed, it raised the mountains over its bed. All was peaceful until one day many years ago the earth trembled with the beast's rage. A roar shook the air. Strong warriors wept and threw away their spears. Children refused to sleep for days. No one spoke for weeks.

"In time, the world went silent again. A great shaman asked a mighty condor to fly over the mountains. The bird returned and spoke of the Pit of Darkness. A great lake of black liquid filled it. When the bird had told all it knew, it fell over dead.

"The great shaman declared that no one should approach the pit. And so we haven't in hundreds of years."

Joran nodded and wiped sweat from his brow. The wiseman's legend matched up with what he'd read about the eruption. The black stuff in the lake had to be bile. Whether the dragon still slept at the bottom of it, he had no idea. Assuming the condor died from bile poisoning, they'd have to be careful not to get too close.

"You have fallen silent, Joran Den Cade," the wiseman said. "I would hear your thoughts."

"I'd like to sort them out myself. Since no one knows if the dragon is still there, I guess we'll need to go and see for ourselves. Of course, if it's sleeping at the bottom of the lake, we still won't know if it's actually there. If we can't confirm the dragon's presence, I won't know how to advise the emperor. Given these facts, I'm not sure what I should do."

"Your situation is difficult. If your enemies seek to wake the beast, who knows what it might do this time. My tribe might be in danger as well. If you choose to continue on your journey, I will send a band to guide you and smooth your passage through the other tribes' lands. All must be warned of the danger anyway."

Joran lowered his gaze in appreciation. "We are grateful for your generosity. Is there somewhere we might sleep? The journey has been a long one."

"There is a cabin we use when emissaries from other tribes visit. You are welcome to it. Food will be brought later."

Joran stood and bowed. "Thank you for your hospitality, sir."

"Ospak." The wiseman stood as well. "We have shared stories and names. You will be considered a friend of the village until you do something to prove you are unworthy. My grandson will guide you to the guest cabin."

Ospak led the way to the door and opened it. A moment later the same group of twelve men came jogging up. A rapid exchange of words ensued and the next thing Joran knew they were being led to another cabin, this one considerably smaller than the first and equally devoid of furniture. Looked like they'd be sleeping on the floor tonight. On the plus side, they had a fireplace and a roof over their head.

After their guides left to find them a meal, Grub got a fire going and they all gathered around. Joran told the dwarves everything Ospak said. When he finished, he added, "All thoughts are welcome."

"I can't figure out why they're being so helpful," Grub said. "We come from the empire. They have to know it's only a matter of time before we send an army to conquer them."

"Do they?" Mia asked. "Given how much we know about them, I figure it's entirely possible they know equally little about us."

"I suspect Mia is right, but that doesn't make Grub's point completely wrong. We are total strangers. Inviting us into their village, offering us a meal and guides, it all seems like too much too soon. At a bare minimum, I plan to check everything they bring for poison. Assuming the food checks out, I'm willing to give the guides the benefit of the doubt. Stoneheart, you've been awfully quiet. Nothing to add?"

"I'm a soldier, my lord. Dealing with things like this..." Stoneheart made a vague gesture at the cabin, but Joran knew what he meant. "I'm not qualified. If we need to fight our way out of here, I'm your man. Otherwise, I'm content to follow your lead."

"Fair enough. At a minimum I want to take a look at the caldera. My fear is that the location combined with the miasma from so much Black Bile will make putting a force in place impossible."

A knock ended the conversation. Mia drew her sword and stepped to one side of the door while Stoneheart went to answer it. One of the villagers Joran hadn't seen before, a girl in her late teens he guessed, carried a steaming iron pot by a loop handle in one hand and a jug in the other.

"Thank you," Joran said. "My friend will take it from there."

She held the containers out and Stoneheart grabbed the iron hoop. Once he had both items she turned and hurried away. This was more what Joran had expected. She seemed properly nervous about total strangers in her village.

Mia closed the door and Stoneheart set the pot and jug on the floor. Joran dug a pouch of upgraded revealing powder out of his kit. In addition to highlighting magic, it also glowed a different color when it touched something poisonous.

He took the lid off the pot and his mouth watered at the savory scent of stew. He really hoped there was no poison as it looked delicious. A quick sprinkle revealed nothing. The food was safe, now for the drink. The powder said it was all good.

Joran smiled, put the revealing powder away, and took out a potion of anti-venom. "If anything happens, force this down my throat."

"You are not trying that food first," Mia said when he offered her the vial.

"Of the four of us, I have the weakest constitution. If I'm

okay, you all will be too. If it comes to a fight, better if I'm the one who's sick. It makes sense and you know that."

"Fine." She snatched the vial out of his hand. "But I don't have to like it."

"True enough." He fished his utensils out of his pack and stabbed a piece of meat first. The venison practically melted in his mouth. "That is so good."

Next he took the jug and sipped the liquid inside. A little bit sweet and a little bit tart. Like cranberries, but less sour. Very tasty regardless.

Mia was staring at him.

"What?"

She drew her sword and held it so the flat faced him. "Smile."

He did so and saw his teeth were stained red from the juice.

"That solves one mystery. If you saw someone after they drank that juice, you might think they'd just drunk blood. Everything seems fine. I say dig in."

Half an hour later all the food was gone and no one had died.

CHAPTER 18

lexandra, along with her family and the imperial guards, exited the long tunnel about a mile outside of Tiber. The opening emerged near the center of a park spared from the axe by royal decree. They found the area deserted, which suited everyone perfectly. Witnesses were to be avoided at all costs. Given that it was the dead of winter, picnickers were not to be found. There weren't even any tracks in the shallow snow.

Though there'd been little choice in the matter, it had come as a relief to find the passage still stable and open after three centuries. Whoever built it knew their business. Her first thought had been the dwarves, but they didn't join the empire until a decade after construction concluded.

Shaking off her useless musings, Alexandra took a moment to brush the worst of the dirt and dust off her robes. The fact that she'd slit the sides to allow for easier movement combined with the grime to make her look more like a beggar than a princess. She did her best to ignore Father and Marcus panting for breath. Octavia just slumped to the grass and closed her eyes. If they were this wiped out now, she didn't know how they'd manage the long walk east. If nothing else, her years in the field had left Alexandra in decent physical shape.

Not that she wouldn't very much prefer a horse.

The guards formed a defensive circle around the exhausted imperial family. Much as she would have liked to let them rest, the more distance they put between themselves and the capital, the better.

A couple minutes passed and she said, "If you can manage it, we need to keep moving. Staying this close to the city is a bad idea."

Father straightened. "Right you are. Though I fear if we leave the park before sunset, we're liable to be spotted."

Alexandra smiled and shook her head. "Since we're dealing with a wizard, I doubt daylight will matter one way or the other. At least with the sun up, we can see where we're going. I don't fancy thrashing through the trees blind."

"Nor do I. Unit Commander, I need men to carry the boys. Everyone else form up in a defensive line. Make due east."

As they got themselves sorted out, a shivering Marcus limped over. Silk slippers were clearly not the best thing for a long hike. "Who's going to carry me? I'm trained for diplomacy, not fieldwork."

Father slapped him on the shoulder. "If I can do it, you can. We need to set an example, not hold everyone up. What will the men think if we can't keep up with Alexandra?"

"Who can?" Marcus asked with seemingly honest confusion.

Father barked a laugh then clamped his jaw shut. "Fair point. Nevertheless, if we don't want to end up dead, we'd best find the strength we need. How far, sweetheart?"

Alexandra considered a moment. "Assuming the enemy didn't attack beyond the palace, there's a garrison ten miles northeast of Tiber at the crossroad where the main trade routes meet. We can collect horses and reinforcements there. And some more appropriate clothes. The imperial family needs to disappear, at least for the time being."

Father's expression turned grim. "I dislike hiding, but until we figure out how to defeat this wizard, I fear you're correct."

"We're ready to go when you are, Your Imperial Majesty," the unit commander said.

"Until I say otherwise, call me 'sir.' Get in the habit. If we want to disguise who we are, you can't be giving us away every time you speak."

"Yes, sir."

Marcus helped Octavia to her feet and the guards formed up around them. The group set out through the forest at a walk. No order had to be given. A blind man could see that Alexandra was the only member of the family capable of better speed at the moment. She debated sending someone ahead, but on the chance that the enemy was hunting for them, she deemed it prudent to keep everyone together.

At least the undergrowth wasn't too heavy and unlike Stello Province, the guards didn't have to cut a path with their swords. Having seen the legions do exactly that plenty of times, she knew how tiring it was.

Alexandra guessed it took most of two hours to make it out of the park and onto the snow-covered dirt path that led to the road. It was packed down hard and the air held enough of a chill that at least they didn't have to walk through mud.

A quick glance left and right confirmed her fear. Octavia and Marcus were nearly done in and Father looked little better. They couldn't be more than three miles from the city with seven more to go. She really didn't want to spend the night out in the open, but given the state of her family, they might not have a choice.

The weary group had barely started down the main trade

route that led to the garrison when the rearmost guard shouted, "Someone's coming up behind us."

Alexandra and the unit commander—she really needed to ask the man's name—hurried back before her father had a chance to order her not to go.

The guards had formed a shield wall across the road two men deep. Alexandra frowned at the ragged figures shuffling toward them. This was no enemy force. If anything, they looked in worse shape than Alexandra's group.

"Halt!" the unit commander bellowed. "Identify yourself!"

A figure in red separated itself and kept coming. A few strides brought him close enough for Alexandra to recognize Cardinal Rufious. "It's okay, he's friendly."

Or as friendly as anyone in the church was to the imperial family.

"Cardinal, you're looking a little worse for wear," she said.

His smile was twisted and held no hint of humor. "I could say the same. Nonetheless, I am pleased to see you alive. Having seen what happened to the palace, His Holiness deemed it prudent to evacuate the church. Would it be possible for us to travel together? We have some White Knights to reinforce you."

"Bring your people up. I'll speak to Father."

"I heard."

She'd been so focused on Rufious she didn't even notice him come up from behind. Some commander she was.

"It's fine. We'll travel to the garrison together and make a plan. At this point, I won't turn down any help to take down that bastard. Between slaughtering everyone at your fortress and sending me fleeing my own palace, he's earned death many times over."

Rufious bowed and went to get the rest of his group.

When he'd gone Father said, "Do you think we can make it tonight?"

Alexandra winced. "The soldiers can, but not at this pace. I didn't want to break up the group, but if we send a runner, the garrison commander can dispatch a wagon."

"To pick up your poor, broken-down father?" His tone held a hint of amusement.

"You're in better shape than Marcus and Octavia. What do you think?"

"At this point, I have no pride left to injure. Unit Commander, send a runner. We'll wait off the road for his return. Perhaps we can have the strategy meeting now."

By the time Septimus reached them, one of the legionnaires was hotfooting it up the road. At that pace he'd reach the garrison in a couple hours.

Father looked the pope up and down when he stood before them and shook his head. His formal white robes were soaked with sweat despite the cold and sticking to his flabby body. His stupid hat had gone by the wayside at some point, leaving his bald head exposed to the sun. Two stunning young women with the dark hair and bronze skin of imperials wearing poorly secured heavy cloaks that gave regular glimpses of their skimpy black-and-white undergarments, kept close to his side and from the looks on their faces they feared he might collapse at any moment.

Oddly, the thought seemed to upset them.

Septimus patted them both on the ass. "Give us some space, ladies."

White Knights and imperial guards made a circle around them, making sure to keep far enough away that they wouldn't be able to eavesdrop. Octavia took the boys a little ways away and the five of them sat on cloaks spread across the snow, clearly done in.

"Any thoughts?" Father asked by way of an opening.

"No." Septimus never looked happy, but today he looked less

happy than usual. "I'm getting thoroughly sick of running for my life. If I never have to do it again, that will suit me fine."

"Agreed," Father said. "We're operating on the assumption that this wizard is the same one that attacked your fortress. Did your knight learn anything that might help us?"

"Did you get a look at him?" Rufious asked.

"I did, though not close up," Alexandra said. "He dressed like a White Knight. Pretty clearly imperial based on his hair and skin tone. He actually matches Joran's description of Samaritan."

"Did his face look melted?"

Alexandra frowned. "Not so far as I could tell. Why?"

"The surviving White Knight indicated that the wizard he saw looked like his face had melted." Rufious scratched his beard. "I wonder if this is the unknown party he speculated about. Though nothing we saw or heard indicates Samaritan has powerful magical abilities."

"Whoever he is," Father said. "We need a way to deal with him. His soldiers are armed with enchanted black swords, but we could overwhelm them with numbers if we had a way to stop the wizard."

Rufious and his master shared a look before Septimus said, "I fear we have nothing to offer beyond the swords of our White Knights."

"What about your now-empty fortress?" Alexandra asked. "We need a new base and that might serve."

"You're welcome to it," Septimus said. "I intend to find a nice quiet church in the middle of nowhere to ride this out. Somewhere no one would ever think of looking for me."

"Oh, no," Father said. "One way or another, you're seeing this through to the end. It's your duty as leader of the church. If you run, so help me, pope or not, I'll kill you myself."

Septimus seemed like he wanted to argue, but Alexandra had

seen that look on Father's face before and knew it would do no good.

The pope seemed to realize it as well. "Fine. We can all die together and the empire with us."

Alexandra didn't care what happened to Septimus, but she intended to see the empire and her family survive no matter what it took.

Their strategy meeting amounted to little and a couple hours before dark two wagons came clattering up the road. Even the heavy supply wagons had no hope of carrying everyone, so half the guards and all the White Knights ended up on foot. Not that they complained. The knights probably saw it as some sort of divine test, and the guards made marches like this all the time during their training and managed it without even getting short of breath.

They reached the garrison fort well after dark. An extremely nervous garrison commander met them in the training yard. He was breathing so fast that Alexandra feared he might faint at Father's approach.

"Welcome, Your Imperial Majesty. How may we be of service?"

"Right now, food and a bed would suit me very well," Father said.

"I need access to your aviary," Alexandra said. "Messages need to be sent."

The commander winced. "We have a limited number of pigeons, though you're welcome to use them all if necessary."

Alexandra hardly needed his permission, but she nodded all the same. Maybe Joran was rubbing off on her.

"Want to get word to your future husband?" Father asked.

"Among others. If Joran returns to the palace, he might end up in trouble. Or at the very least confused that we're not there. The other legions need to be alerted as well. Hopefully tomorrow we'll spot the dragon ship. That'll get us where we're going far faster than a wagon."

"Indeed. Join us when you're finished." Father led the others toward the keep.

When they'd gone, a nervous young legionnaire approached. "I can show you to the aviary, Majesty."

"Thank you." Yes, Joran was definitely rubbing off on her. For better or worse she had yet to decide.

CHAPTER 19

Beastmaster appeared in the clearing near the stupid fortress where they found the artifact holding Khashair. At least this close to the ocean, the worst of the winter cold was held off. It saved him the tiny bit of magic he'd need to keep himself warm.

Fane told him to come here, find the mechanism that controlled the flow of Black Bile, and shut it off. Neither of them had any idea what it looked like, though he did have the map with him which should help.

He was getting thoroughly sick of running her errands. He had his own experiments to conduct. It wasn't like he just sat around in the tunnels playing fetch with the weasels all day. Not that Fane cared.

Shaking his head, Beastmaster turned toward the ocean and took to the air. Walking would take too long, but he'd eventually need to land and search on foot.

The flight lasted only minutes and then he was hovering over the glittering blue water. Waves lapped against a sheer cliff that dropped a good hundred feet. The forest ended a hundred yards before the cliff, but he saw nothing interesting in the empty corridor, just weeds and shrubs.

A quick consultation with the map didn't really tell him much. It wasn't to scale, had no references beyond mentioning the cliff, and was centuries out of date.

He stuck the atlas back in his satchel and stared through the ether. The controls had to run on magic. Maybe if he flew around and checked he'd spot something interesting. He might complain about her orders, but Beastmaster really didn't want to have to go back and explain that he failed to find anything. Fane was hard enough to deal with when she wasn't angry. Bringing bad news only made her worse.

He flew south first, checking for surges in the ether, black iron, or anything else out of the ordinary. Ten miles passed, twenty, and still nothing. If he wasn't immortal, Beastmaster would have resented this mission even more. As it was, boredom seemed his greatest threat.

You shouldn't say things like that, even in your head. Nothing good ever happened to someone that thought they were safe.

As if some demon had read his mind, a surge of corrupt energy appeared ahead of him.

Beastmaster dropped straight down.

An instant later a lance of black energy streaked through the space he'd just occupied.

He traced the attack back to a black iron rod jutting three feet out of the ground. It was already gathering energy for another blast.

That wouldn't do at all.

Beastmaster forged an ethereal construct shaped like a hand, grabbed the rod, and yanked.

A burst of energy destroyed his spell before it even budged the rod.

Okay, plan B. He blasted the earth around it, sending giant clods flying.

Another blast lanced in, forcing him to dive out of the way.

His attack revealed a piece of black iron running north and south connected to the rod. The beam crackled with corruption.

"That's the power source," he muttered. "So how do I disconnect it?"

Beastmaster hated magical engineering, that's why he worked with animals. Warping flesh was so much simpler.

He danced around another blast. At least the thing had lousy aim.

When in doubt, fire tended to do the trick.

He rubbed his thumb and forefinger together and combined the heat with ether. A white-hot lance of fire shot out, hitting the base of the rod. He kept the stream up for ten seconds before the rod finally fell over.

A minute passed and nothing shot at him. Seemed safe enough now. He landed for a closer look.

The rod was nothing special, probably worked like a wand to focus and sort of aim the magic. Didn't really work very well, but considering how old it was, the fact that it worked at all impressed him.

Shifting his focus to the underground beam, he found it still coursing with corruption. With any luck he could follow that right back to the source. He'd just have to be careful to watch for more emitters.

Flying as high as possible while still keeping the stream of corruption in sight, Beastmaster headed south. Two more black iron rods popped up on his journey, but now that he knew how to deal with them, they posed no particular threat.

Half a mile later he reached the end of the rail. The problem was there was nothing there. The line of corruption just stopped. There was no tower, no fortress, no nothing. He turned toward the ocean. No sign of anything having fallen over the cliff.

Standing in midair, hands on hips, Beastmaster cursed the universe in general and unreasonable vampires in particular. What was he supposed to do now?

The answer came a moment later when a circle of dirt opened like a clamshell and a man made of black iron climbed out. He looked closer. Not a man, a golem of some sort. Maybe it could tell him about the mechanism.

He pointed and a tentacle of ether shot out to wrap up the golem.

As soon as it touched the figure's metal skin, the spell shattered.

The metal man looked up at him. Beastmaster looked back. They stared at each other. The attack he expected never came.

Time to try something less direct. Instead of targeting the golem directly, he blasted the dirt at its feet and lifted it up on a disk of compressed earth. Quick as he could, Beastmaster flew out over the ocean. At a hundred yards from shore he stopped. Looked nice and deep here.

"Can you talk?" he asked.

It stared at him until Beastmaster was about ready to dump it in the drink then finally said, "You are a trespasser. By command of the overmages, you must be slain."

It had a weird, inhuman voice. Not deep or gravelly like a demon. He'd never heard anything like it.

"How are you going to manage that?"

The golem stared at him again for an uncomfortably long time then said, "You are a trespasser. By command of the overmages, you must be slain."

"Wow. And I thought the archbishop's overseers were dumb. You make them look like geniuses. I'm going to go take a look around your place. Have a nice swim."

"You are a—"

Beastmaster released the spell holding the earthen disk together and the golem fell with a huge splash into the ocean. That probably wouldn't destroy it, but it would give him plenty of time to explore before it dragged itself out.

He landed beside the open hatch and looked down. An iron ladder led into the darkness. That was no particular problem for him as he saw nearly as well in the dark as he did in broad daylight. No wards crackled in the ether waiting to blast him and physical traps seemed unlikely.

Whatever, he wanted to get this done sooner rather than later.

Not bothering with the ladder, he flew down and hovered just above the floor. Just in case there were pit traps, this would be much safer.

The tunnel ran straight ahead. Unlike his tunnels, these were perfectly square and smooth. There were no seams visible and everything was made out of black iron. The empire certainly lived up to its name.

He expected the tunnel to branch at some point, but it ran dead straight for about fifty yards before stopping at a closed door made of more black iron. There was no handle. How did you open the stupid thing?

Just to be safe, he conjured an ethereal construct and guided it to the door. As soon as it touched, the spell shattered.

"So you work just like that stupid golem."

He settled on the floor in front of the door and gingerly put his hand on the metal.

No reaction.

Muttering curses under his breath, Beastmaster searched all around the door. He'd almost given up hope when he touched a particular section of wall and it slid up out of sight. Underneath he found nine stone squares set into the wall and marked with the magic-resisting symbols the empire liked to use. At least these were easy to figure out; each square had a mark that corresponded to a number, one through nine.

There had to be a code that opened the door, but he hadn't the least idea what it might be. Maybe Fane would know.

Time to head back and talk to her.

Beastmaster retraced his steps and emerged from the hatch. Not wanting it to seal again, he blasted it with flames until the hinge melted. A quick yank pulled it free and he tossed it into the ocean.

There, now at least they'd be able to get back in. He marked the location with an ethereal rune and teleported home.

He barely had a chance to orient himself before Fane said, "Did you find it?"

Beastmaster slowly turned to find her standing in the doorway of his throne room. "I found something. But whatever I found is locked behind a black iron door and I don't know the code to open it."

"Just blast it open."

"Can't. Magic won't touch it. That's why I came back. Figured you might have an idea."

"If magic won't work, maybe brute force will. You marked the entrance?"

"Of course."

"Okay. Once the sun sets, we'll go back and see about forcing it open."

He nodded, less than thrilled about having to go back, but still pleased that she didn't seem too upset. With Fane, that was about the best you could hope for.

————

Fane appeared on the cliffside Beastmaster marked and found him waiting for her. That showed a bit of initiative, a rare thing for him. She'd taken the time to visit her citadel before coming here. One of her remaining Hell-forged swords rode in a sheath strapped to her back. If she couldn't hack her way in with this, then they had no hope of gaining access to the control room. Assuming that was even what waited behind the door.

"Brought one of your treasures I see. Shall we give it a try?"

She didn't bother to respond, instead flying down into the tunnel. Everything appeared exactly as he described. Fane spent a moment studying the symbols, even going so far as to apply a little ether to try and coax them into revealing their meaning. To her surprise they yielded right away. Though all she learned was that they meant one through nine, exactly as Beastmaster had guessed.

Time to get down to business. She reached back and drew the sword from its sheath. A quick glance over her shoulder confirmed that Beastmaster was keeping his distance. Good, that would keep him out of her way. Fane didn't expect a violent reaction, but just because she didn't expect it, didn't mean there wouldn't be one.

Ether coursed through her body, strengthening her already supernaturally powerful muscles. She added a shield to that and swung with all her might.

The Hell-forged blade slammed into the door with a horrendous screech. It cut a foot-long gash in the lesser metal. The door looked to be about six inches thick. Less than she'd feared, but still plenty heavy-duty. The gap she made was about a finger wide, plenty for her.

She sheathed the sword and turned to Beastmaster. "Keep watch out here, I'm going in."

Not waiting for a reply, she called on one of the powers she gained along with her undead form and dissolved into a gray mist. A couple seconds later she reformed and looked around the modest-sized room. There really wasn't much beyond a strange desk. The top was tilted about sixty degrees, and glowing runes covered it. Runes like the ones on the door panel that she couldn't read.

On the wall above the table, a glowing rectangle was covered with black lines and circles. Now that looked familiar. She snapped her fingers. It perfectly matched the pipe diagram Beastmaster brought back. That had to mean the runes were the key to controlling the bile network.

Now if only she could read them.

Slowly, gently, Fane sent ether through the runes then back into her eyes. As she expected, they resisted. And unlike Beastmaster, she didn't dare brute force them. If she used too much power and erased the runes, she'd have no hope of draining the pipes and defeating Khashair.

Time meant nothing to her as she massaged the runes. Eventually one of them wavered and shimmered until it read, "northwest connection six."

She blew out a long breath, a force of habit from her days among the living, and blinked her blurry eyes. When they cleared, she looked up at the glowing rectangle and found the tiny matching rune on a red circle. That wasn't too far from Beastmaster's tunnels.

With an ethereal brand, she burned the symbol and its translation into the floor. Now all she needed to do was translate the rest. There couldn't be more than a few hundred.

She swallowed a hysterical laugh. One of the good things about being undead, she could work day and night with only short breaks to restore herself. No matter how long it took, she'd sort this out.

And when she did, Khashair would pay for his arrogance.

CHAPTER 20

Joran sat beside Mia in the back of a sleigh drawn by reindeer. One of the village warriors assigned to guide them—he'd spoken so fast that the translation potion garbled his name—to the mountains and warn the other tribes sat in the front seat and handled the reins with expert skill. It seemed this was the preferred method of traveling during the winter. Joran certainly found no fault with it. At the very least it beat walking and allowed them to make good time on their journey. With any luck they'd finish the mission and be back even sooner than his most optimistic guess.

He pulled the black bearskin blanket up higher on his chest. Between it and his enchanted cloak, the freezing weather almost felt cozy. Hopefully Stoneheart and Grub were equally comfortable in the sleigh behind them. More likely they were entertaining themselves by bickering like an old married couple.

"When do you think we'll reach the last village?" Joran asked.

Without looking back the driver said, "Before sunset. We'll sleep there and set out for the Pit of Darkness at dawn."

Joran would certainly be glad to spend the night in one of

the cozy cabins. Lean-tos dug into the snow didn't exactly make for comfortable sleeping.

He leaned back and closed his eyes, letting the swish of the skis lull his mind. It didn't help. At the best of times Joran had a hard time turning off his brain and this was far from that.

"You're thinking hard again," Mia said. "Want to share?"

"I finally figured out why the people here seem a little off to me. It's their openness. They go into a meeting thinking we're going to be friends until proven otherwise. That's basically the exact opposite of an imperial noble. They assume you're trying to figure out how best to use them and then do their best to take advantage of you first. I prefer this way." He turned his head enough to see her. "We also need a better name for this place than the Land of the Blood Drinkers."

"How about the Land of the Reindeer Herders?"

"That's good, but I fear the generals will reject it as insufficiently threatening. Pity we don't have time to work out some sort of treaty that brings them into the empire peacefully. I've come to like these people and have no desire to see them harmed."

"Maybe when things settle down you can offer to do for them what you did for the lizardmen in Stello Province."

"We can hope."

They spent the rest of the trip in comfortable silence and about half an hour before sunset, the village came into view. Unlike the last ones they'd visited, this village had a proper, ten-foot-tall stockade fence topped with spikes. Guards armed with spears marched around the catwalk, seeming alert.

"This is different," Mia said.

Joran nodded. He didn't like finding such a serious fortification around one of the villages. It implied trouble, and this close to the pit he refused to believe it was only a coincidence.

The sleigh stopped in front of the closed gate and their guide climbed down. He looked back at them. His eyes were narrow and his brow furrowed. "Wait here."

"What's going on?" Joran asked.

He shook his head. "No idea. The wall wasn't here when last we came to visit."

With that their guide turned back and strode up to the wall.

"He's scared," Mia said. "Did you notice how stiff he walked?"

"Yes, and his expression was about as grim as I've seen on anyone, much less these people. I fear we've found trouble."

"What else is new?"

The second sleigh pulled up beside theirs and Stoneheart stood up. "What's going on?"

"Our guide is attempting to find that out as we speak. Clearly these people have run into some trouble. Hopefully that trouble won't impact our mission."

"And if it does?" Grub asked.

"Then we deal with it as necessary. These people have been generous with us. If we can do something for them in return, it's our responsibility to do so, though not at the expense of our mission."

Five minutes later their driver jogged back, his expression smooth once more. "They've been attacked off and on by creatures coming down out of the mountains. It started two years ago. There have been deaths, but none since they put up the wall. I convinced them to let us enter and speak to their wiseman."

Two broad-shouldered blond men dressed in heavy furs pushed the doors open and beckoned them through. A flick of the reins got the sleigh moving and soon enough they were through.

The sleigh had barely stopped when a shout rang out from behind them.

Everyone leapt out and ran for the gate. The guards were

fending off a quartet of...somethings. While Joran tried to figure out what the black-furred things were, Mia drew her mithril sword and sprinted into the fray.

The guards seemed to be having trouble with their iron-tipped spears not penetrating the beasts' fur.

Mia's mithril sword cut through them with the same ease it cut through everything else.

Before Stoneheart could even join the fight, all four creatures were dead.

"She makes me feel useless," the dwarf muttered.

"Don't. Mia was one of the finest warriors in the empire before adding a soul bond and a mithril sword. I doubt there's a mortal being out there that can match her."

The guards were offering their thanks in the rapid-fire fashion favored by the people of this country. Mia looked bemused, but she kept up her smile and nodded along. She also kept her sword out just in case more of those things showed up.

Smart girl.

Joran hurried over to help. "Gentlemen, would it be possible to bring one of those things inside? I'd like to take a closer look, preferably with the gate closed."

Their faces twisted up in distaste, but one of them said, "Very well, though no one here has succeeded in making heads or tails of them."

Mia and Stoneheart worked together to drag one of them in before the guards closed and secured the gate with a beam. The beast was bigger than the biggest wolf he'd ever seen. Joran knelt for a closer look.

The fur looked almost wet and not with blood. "Mia, would you touch your sword to its fur?"

She obliged him with her usual good nature. The instant the mithril blade touched its fur, it started to hiss and steam. Just as he expected. This thing was like the serpent, some sort of bile-mutated beast. Perhaps it fell into the pit.

No, that didn't make sense. The bile would have killed it before it transformed. Someone must have done this, but who and why? Hopefully the dragon itself wasn't involved. That would mean that it was awake.

He shook his head. Maybe the wiseman would know something.

Joran straightened and frowned. As he watched, the beast melted into a puddle of sludge that quickly soaked into the ground and vanished from sight.

"Did you expect it to do that?" Mia asked.

"No. Thanks for your help."

"Happy to. And I'm glad I got there in time to save those men."

"As am I. But I can't figure out how they fend the beasts off if their weapons can't pierce the monsters' hides. I mean, a pointed stick would be as effective as those spears."

Off to one side, their guide was busy having a rapid-fire conversation with a group of warriors. Joran made no effort to listen in. He'd quickly learned that trying to hear multiple voices upset the translation potion and gave him a headache. Given what just happened, he suspected he'd need all his focus when they finally got to talk to the wiseman.

"How come we never run into normal things?" Grub asked. "Since we started traveling together, we've fought demons, talking statues, and mutated beasts. How about some bandits for The One God's sake?"

"We fought dwarf rebels," Stoneheart said. "That's pretty close to bandits."

Before an argument could start, their guide strode over and said, "They offer their thanks for your help with the black hounds. The village wiseman will speak to you now."

He led the group to a log cabin that rested in the center of the village. It was the largest though Joran would have bet gold that it had only one room. It seemed every village was laid out exactly the same. Why that should be he hadn't the slightest idea. Part of him wanted to ask, but the larger part pointed out that they had more pressing business and that he shouldn't get off track.

The man that met them at the door of the cabin looked like a lad compared to the first wiseman, though Joran guessed his age at over sixty. He wore leathers and had the build of a warrior: broad shoulders, massive chest, and arms bigger than Joran's legs. He offered them a wide smile and waved them in.

Inside the fire was blessedly modest and even better a table with proper chairs sat in front of it. Joran certainly didn't consider himself too good to sit on the floor, but he did find a chair more comfortable. These even had cushions.

When everyone had taken a seat to their liking Joran said, "Thank you for letting us enter your village. My name is Joran Den Cade."

Joran introduced the rest of his companions and the wiseman said, "I'm Thordin and I offer my thanks for slaying the black hounds. Those are the first of the miserable beasts anyone has killed."

"Meaning no disrespect to your warriors, but having seen how ineffective their weapons are against the monsters, I can't help wondering how you fended them off."

"With difficulty. The wall helps, though they do try and climb it. The only reason the beasts haven't killed us all is that they die after about an hour then turn into that black sludge which vanishes into the ground. It does so even in the heart of winter when the earth is frozen harder than stone. Now my question. Why do you seek the Pit of Darkness?"

Joran explained their concerns without going into the full details. "I need to find out what's there and how we might best keep our enemy from reaching it and unleashing the dragon's wrath on all of us."

Thordin's frown turned his face into a mass of crags and

wrinkles. "We've never seen a dragon and since the attacks, none of my people have dared enter the mountains. Given the creatures wandering the passes, I advise you to give up on your mission. Anyone foolish enough to attempt to reach the pit will be torn to pieces by them."

If Joran could be sure that would be the result of Samaritan's quest, he would be happy to do as the wiseman suggested. "Thank you for your advice. Would it be possible for us to spend the night here? If we're to continue our mission, I would just as soon do it after a good night's sleep."

"You're perfectly welcome. Under better circumstances, I would arrange a feast to welcome you, but now is not the time for a distraction."

They were quickly guided to a guest cabin while their guides ended up staying with some warriors that they knew from previous visits. Once the fire was going, the group gathered around to plan their next move. Well, technically Joran was planning their next move. Everyone else just looked at him for orders.

"What do you guys think?" he asked without great optimism that they'd share an opinion.

To his surprise Grub said, "If it's as bad in the mountains as he made out, I say we call our mission done and report back. Getting a legion out here's going to be damn near impossible anyway."

"Much as it pains me to agree," Stoneheart said. "The logistics are too much even for the empire. And I can't imagine imperial steel being any more effective against those things than iron. The alchemists might be able to do something about them, but we'd still need to arrange food and supplies for several thousand men."

"I doubt even the Iron Princess could figure it out," Mia added.

Joran blew out a breath. "Alright. Let's call it a night. We'll see what circumstances dictate in the morning and if nothing's changed, we'll head for home."

———

J oran drifted through darkness. He had to be dreaming since he didn't know how to fly. Not that he'd ever dreamed about flying before. Which was strange since from what others said, it was a common subject.

He tried to will himself somewhere, but nothing happened. So it was going to be one of those dreams, where he had no control and just had to wait for it to end. Usually, he wasn't this aware of the dreams he couldn't control.

With no other option he shrugged and waited to see what his subconscious would throw at him.

The answer came seconds later when a pair of golden eyes as big as he was tall appeared directly in front of him. They glowed with an inner light and had vertical pupils. As far as dreams went, this was one of the odder ones he'd ever had.

"This isn't a dream," a deep but not unkind voice said. "I chose this moment to speak with you so we wouldn't be interrupted. I am this world's guardian dragon."

Joran stared. "So you are awake. From what I've heard and read, I assumed you were more of the 'smash first and talk later' sort. I'm pleased to find you more reasonable."

"The angel told you that dragons were made of the mingled blood of The Creator and The Destroyer. I am mostly Destroyer. What you are speaking to now is the tiny fragment of Creator essence in me. The Destroyer part sleeps and I would keep it so. Once the greater part of me is roused, I lose all influence and it will go on a rampage."

"Like what happened in the Black Iron Empire?"

"Yes, though that was no great loss to this world. Since we

want the same thing, I hoped we might come to an understanding."

"I would be delighted to do so," Joran said. "All I wish is to see my empire safe and secure. It is far from perfect, but there are good people in it. Do you know who's sending the beasts to attack this village?"

"I am. I wish to keep people away from my sleeping body. This village sent men into the mountains; though they kept their distance, they were still too close for my liking. I hoped they might take the hint and relocate. When they built a wall instead, I decided they needed to be destroyed."

Joran chewed his lip. Second-guessing a dragon might not be the best idea, but he'd give it a shot anyway. "These are good people and they already consider your home taboo. None of them will go there and if I explain the circumstances, I'm sure I can convince them to warn away anyone that might think of exploring the area as well as keeping their warriors out of the mountains."

"I sense the truth of your words. Tell them to never set foot in the mountains again. I will pull my beasts that far back. If they do not break the terms of this deal, I will not."

"I think Thordin will accept those terms." Joran rubbed his eyes. "Is your dark side so easy to wake?"

"No. The only reason those idiot overmages did it was because, in trying to control me, they suppressed The Creator side which freed The Destroyer side. Only an exceedingly powerful wizard or group of wizards could do that. But after what happened last time, I refuse to take any chances. Warn them and keep your distance. Together we may keep my Destroyer side asleep forever."

Joran bowed to the golden eyes. "Nothing would please me more. Is there anything else I can do to help?"

"Keeping these people away from me is enough. It pained me

to have to slay them, but not nearly as much as wiping out a continent would have." The eyes faded away.

Joran waited for them to reappear, but they never did.

————

J oran woke feeling perfectly well rested despite his odd conversation with the dragon. The idea of a dragon with a split personality was at once bizarre and terrifying in roughly equal measure. On the other hand, knowing that the dragon wasn't pure evil and that a part of it was trying to do the right thing made him feel a good deal better about the empire's situation.

The fire had burned down to almost nothing, leaving the cabin chilly. He added a few sticks from the pile of firewood beside the hearth. A little magical coaxing had it roaring soon enough.

"Are you okay?" Mia was staring him from her spot on the floor nearby.

"Why do you ask?" He held his hands out and rubbed them together.

"Something weird happened last night. I don't know what, but you woke me up. When I checked, you looked sound asleep."

Joran told her about the dream. "You must have caught the edge of it through our link. Anyway, I hope Thordin will prove reasonable."

"Everything we've seen indicates these are the most reasonable people we've ever met. If you explain how it stops those monsters from attacking his village, I bet he'll be anxious to do what the dragon wants."

The group had barely finished breakfast when someone knocked on the door. Thordin and a pair of warriors waited outside. Having no desire to let more cold air in than necessary,

Joran waved them in. Before settling around the table, he drank a fresh translation potion.

"Did you have a good night?" Thordin asked.

"I had an interesting night." Joran told him about the dream conversation. "So as long as you stay out of the mountains, the monsters won't attack the village."

"I dislike being told where I can and can't go, but not nearly as much as I hate seeing my warriors killed by those creatures. We only go to hunt mountain goats anyway. Staying out will be no great trial. What I don't understand is why the dragon didn't speak to me directly."

Joran shrugged. "The topic didn't come up. All I can think of is that it sensed Mia kill some of its creations then discovered our intention to explore the pit. The combination may have been enough to prompt it to speak. That's pure speculation on my part. Figuring out the mind of a dragon is far beyond my abilities."

Thordin chuckled. "True enough. Now that you have spoken to the beast, what will you do?"

"Go home and report to the emperor. There's nothing we can do that will make a difference beyond killing the man that's so desperate to wake the dragon. Before we leave, I'd like to ask your opinion about something. Do you think the tribes would be willing to join the empire? Very little about your lives would change save the addition of merchants and priests to your daily lives. It would save a great deal of bloodshed when the empire eventually turns its gaze west."

"My people are strong and independent. Bowing to any power, much less an outside one, will not be done lightly. That said, we have no desire to fight a meaningless war. When the time comes, bring us your terms and we will discuss them. I make no promises beyond that."

Joran smiled and held out his hand. "I can ask for nothing

more. Were it my decision, we wouldn't even consider invading another nation, but, alas, it isn't up to me."

They shook on it and an hour later Joran and his companions were on their way southeast. With the sleighs to carry them and no need to make more stops, the journey should be over in short order. He had no idea what was happening in Tiber, but he badly wanted to see Alexandra.

CHAPTER 21

Alexandra sat in the back of the supply wagon beside her father. They both wore standard legion tunics and trousers and neither of them looked anything like who they were. In fact, Father looked like a grizzled commander and when she spotted him earlier, Marcus might have passed for a rookie unit commander. At least he had boots now instead of slippers. The real problem was her, Octavia, and the boys. None of them blended in. Alexandra especially was well known to everyone as the Iron Princess.

Oh well, you did the best you could and hoped it was enough. The fact that they were still alive meant they'd done something right. At least she hoped they'd done something right and it wasn't just that the wizard hadn't come looking for them yet.

What they hadn't done, despite regular discussions, was come up with a plan anyone thought had a hope in hell of defeating the wizard. It was a horrible feeling and she wanted it to end as quickly as possible.

What she wanted even more was to see Joran. She missed his

steady, reassuring presence. If he were here, surely he'd have come up with an idea by now.

"Copper for your thoughts," Father said.

"Nothing useful, just the same things going around in circles. If we live through this, we really need to invest in training wizards of our own. We're too helpless as it is."

"You'll get no argument from me and I doubt Septimus will utter a word of protest either. Some of the more devout might have an issue with it, but they'll adapt, quickly."

She hoped it would be that simple.

"Dragon ship approaching!" one of the imperial guards said.

Alexandra sprang to her feet in the back of the wagon. "Stop. I need to signal them."

The driver reined in and Alexandra drew the imperial steel dagger she'd had polished to a mirror shine for just this moment. There was a special code known only to the dragon ship captains and the imperial family. It wasn't long, but it was precise. Every captain knew that when he saw that signal, regardless of his mission, he stopped and lowered the gondola as close as possible to where he saw it.

She flashed the signal and waited.

A minute passed with no change in the ship's course.

She tried again and this time, seconds later, the sails moved and the ship came right toward them. Good, he must have just missed it the first time. She sheathed the dagger and everyone climbed out of the wagons.

"We're going to have to leave some of them behind," Alexandra said. "The ship is already overloaded with alchemists and White Knights."

"How many can we take?" Father asked.

"Half the guards along with Rufious and the pope. I'd just as soon not take that many, but I don't want to leave the guards behind. If we need to fight, they're the best we have."

"I trust your judgement. Give the orders. I need to talk to your brother before we go."

Alexandra frowned but nodded. What could he have to say to Marcus that they hadn't already said? She shrugged and went to find Unit Commander Ligur. The guard commander had blushed to his ears when she asked his name. Holding back a giggle at his reaction had taken a great deal of self-control.

As she expected, he stood at the head of the column, eyes alert for any threat. He spotted her at once and all the men snapped to attention. "Princess?"

"We're transferring over to the dragon ship. I want you to pick twenty of your best men. Much as I'd like to take them all, we don't have room for everyone."

"Understood, Majesty." He bowed and started barking orders.

Alexandra had long since given up trying to convince everyone to stop calling her by her title. When it came to the legionnaires, she was the Iron Princess and that was it. Sometimes she thought they considered her their leader even more than Father. The imperial guards were usually better, but they were all drafted from the legions and old habits died hard.

By the time the dragon ship lowered its gondola, everyone had gathered to board. Father arrived last, but she saw no sign of her brother.

"Where's Marcus and his family?"

"They're not coming. If worst comes to worst, I don't want every member of the royal family gathered in one place. Should we fall, at least Marcus will survive to continue the fight."

Alexandra raised an eyebrow at that.

"I know, he's not ready. That's as much my fault for babying him as it is his for not stepping up more. Hopefully it doesn't come to that."

She heartily agreed with that sentiment. If the fate of the

empire rested on Marcus's shoulders, she shuddered to think how things would turn out.

———

M arcus trembled slightly as the final gondola filled with imperial guards ascended to the dragon ship. He wanted, more than almost anything he'd ever wanted up to this moment in his life, to be on the ship with Father and Alexandra. He understood very well Father's reasons for making him stay behind. Having the family in one place would make them easier to wipe out should the wizard learn their location.

But though he understood it, that didn't mean he agreed it was a good idea. Marcus had a thorough understanding of his strengths and weaknesses. Inspirational leadership in the face of a great danger didn't number among his strengths. He had serious doubts it ever would. If the threat was too much paper-work or a disgruntled nobleman, Marcus felt he was the best person in the empire to deal with it. Military matters, even small-scale ones, not so much.

Octavia slipped up beside him and put her hand in his. "We'll be alright and so will they. You're stronger than you believe."

"You always were a sweet talker." He kissed her cheek. "How are the boys holding up?"

"Marcus is having a ball. He thinks it's all a big adventure. Vel isn't sure what to make of it all, but he's doing okay so far. I don't know how he'll do if there's a battle, but for now, both of them are okay."

"Thank The One God for small favors." Marcus wiped sweat from his brow. Despite the cold he found himself drenched.

"Sir?" The garrison commander approached, looking a bit nervous.

Marcus straightened and did his best to look less nervous than he felt. Shouldn't be too hard given how much time he spent faking it. Octavia gave his hand a final squeeze before walking back to their wagon.

"What is it?" he asked.

"Do you have orders for us?"

His job, until he knew otherwise, was to stay alive. Simple enough as long as the wizard didn't get wind of his location. "Let's head back to the garrison. Until we hear from Father and Alexandra, we'll be staying with you and your command. You and your men will keep to your regular schedule. No one watching will have any idea my family and I are there. If, The One God forbid, the worst happens and Father and Alexandra fall in battle, you will help me rally the legions to avenge them."

The garrison commander's gulp was audible from three strides away.

"I share that sentiment. None of us are ready, but that doesn't matter. We must all do our duty to the best of our ability. I'll be counting on you."

The garrison commander straightened and looked Marcus in the eye. "You can count on me, sir."

Marcus clapped him on the shoulder. Now if he could find some of that courage, maybe they'd come through this alive.

He sent a silent prayer to any power watching that it didn't come to that.

CHAPTER 22

Beastmaster lay on the cold tunnel floor and stared up at the blank ceiling. How long had Fane been in there? He'd lost track, but far too long for his liking. His job, according to her, was to make sure no one bothered her while she worked. Who, exactly, she imagined bothering her down here, he had no idea. At least she'd let him teleport home to eat and feed the prisoner.

He briefly debated not coming back, but rejected the idea. Boring though it might be, as an immortal, Beastmaster had all the time in the world to make up for it. If he disobeyed Fane, boredom would be the least of his problems. Sometimes, in the very back of his mind, he wondered whether rooting for Khashair might not make more sense. But he always came back to the same truth: better the devil you know.

A little shriek of frustration came from inside the control room. She let one out every few hours. He assumed when one of the runes proved especially stubborn. At least she hadn't blown anything up yet. Beastmaster took that as a good sign.

Several dull clanks sounded from the entrance. Beastmaster sat up in time to see a dripping-wet black statue reach the bottom of the stairs. He grinned. Took the stupid thing long enough to get back here.

"You are a trespasser. By command of the overmages, you must be slain."

Beastmaster shook his head. This guy needed to learn some new lines.

The golem's eyes flashed red and a vibration ran through the floor. Ten niches, five on either side of the passage, started to slide up into the ceiling. He caught a glimpse of black iron feet before jumping up from the floor and running to the control room.

"We've got a problem out here."

"Deal with it! I'm almost done."

"There are eleven magic-proof golems in the hall. How, exactly, do you expect me to deal with them?"

He caught the sound of muffled footsteps then the Hell-forged black iron sword popped out of the gash in the door. It clanged on the floor before he could catch it.

"Take that and don't bother me again."

Beastmaster picked up the sword and winced when it stung his hand. He was neither a warrior nor an undead, so why was she giving him a Hell-forged sword he didn't know how to use? He'd held swords before, though not since he was an actual kid and he'd certainly never wielded one in battle.

First time for everything.

The niche doors clunked into place and the golems stepped into the hall before turning to face him. As one they said, "You are a trespasser. By command of the overmages, you must be slain."

Beastmaster wrapped his hands in ether and the stinging went away. Next, he infused his body with power. He might not be a warrior, but you didn't have to be a genius to swing a sword.

He kicked the ground and rushed toward the nearest golem.

He swung with all his might and hacked its leg off at the knee.

That went pretty well.

His enhanced speed saved him from a backhand that would have caved his head in.

Right, can't get distracted in the middle of a fight.

Swinging like mad, his body powered by ether, Beastmaster dispatched the first four golems in seconds. He left their parts on the floor and moved on.

The iron men did their best to stop him, but they were too slow and stupid to keep up with him. Against a normal opponent, he had no doubt they'd make quick work of them. Against him, they were more annoyance than threat.

At least they broke the monotony.

Two minutes after his first swing, all but the original golem lay unmoving on the floor. Golem One's eyes flashed red and Beastmaster feared more reinforcements would be on the way, but nothing happened.

They stared at each other for a few seconds then Beastmaster got bored, sprinted in, and hacked the golem's legs off.

It crashed to the floor. "You are a—"

A final hard blow separated its head from its neck.

He wiped the sweat from his brow and released his spells. He hadn't been in a real fight for a long time. It was kind of fun. Maybe he'd have to try joining his pets when they went hunting.

Out of curiosity he went to the nearest niche and glanced inside. Nothing there beyond a circle of those unreadable runes on the floor. They crackled in his magical vision. Probably some kind of sustaining spell for the golems. Not his area of expertise, but he knew enough about golem crafting to understand the basic principles.

He debated reporting in and immediately dismissed the idea. She said not to bother her and he had no intention of disobeying. He'd gotten yelled at enough for one day.

Beastmaster grinned at the many pieces of golem littering the floor. Maybe he could at least make himself a chair out of all this mess.

———

F ane's lips twisted in barely controlled rage with each crash as Beastmaster hacked the golems to pieces. There were only ten runes left to decode. She was so close, but how could anyone concentrate with all that racket? Not that there was a quiet way to cut through metal, but couldn't he at least hurry up? She wanted this done and then she wanted to find Khashair and take out all her frustration on him.

Without his precious power boost, the arrogant overmage would quickly find out which of them held the greatest power. Fane was very much looking forward to ripping his head off and feeding it to her undead slaves.

When a few seconds passed without a clash of metal she let out a breath. He was finally done.

Turning her attention back to the control panel, she started coaxing one of the remaining runes. It resisted at first, but she had plenty of practice translating them and after a few seconds it yielded its meaning. Finding an unmarked spot of the floor to burn the translation was getting to be a bigger challenge than actually translating.

Three tedious hours later Fane was done. She knew what every rune meant. Now, how to shut off the flow of bile?

First, she needed to drain the pipes and surface pits into the underground lakes or "lagoons" as the runes called them. She touched the rune marked "drain" and watched the glowing map. Seconds passed and nothing happened.

That had been the correct rune, she knew it. So why didn't it work?

Fane looked around again for some instructions, but there

was nothing beyond the rune-marked control panel. No doubt whichever lackey ran this place would've already known how to activate the runes.

She tried holding her finger on the rune with equally poor results. Snarling and baring her fangs, she sent a burst of ether into the rune. Either the damn thing would activate or she'd burn it out. At this point, she'd had enough screwing around.

Happily, the ether flowed into the rune, it glowed red, and the board above lit up. It seemed to be working, but there was only one way to be sure.

Closing her eyes, she sent her sight soaring up and out of the control room. She hissed at the bright daylight, but it didn't actually hurt her ethereal construct. Fane had explored around here before during her search for the Black Iron Empire's capital. It took only a moment to orient herself and fly back down into the earth.

She stuck her insubstantial eyes into a pipe and found it flowing with bile. Flying along with the flow, she reached a lagoon and watched as bile poured in from a number of pipes. Looked like the system was working just like she wanted.

Good. Now all she needed to do was wait. Once the pipes had fully drained, she'd hunt down Khashair and then they'd find out for real which of them was stronger.

CHAPTER 23

The sleigh carrying Joran, Mia, and their guide slowed to a stop about two miles from the imperial border. They'd made good time despite a late-season snow storm two days ago. Four inches of fresh powder didn't trouble the reindeer in the least.

Despite their guide's offer to take them right to the fort, Joran deemed it best not to let Commander Ramirus see them with the locals. It would bring questions he had no desire to answer before talking to Alexandra and the emperor. Hopefully they'd be pleased to hear the empire didn't have a hostile civilization on its western border.

"Is that our dragon ship?" Mia asked.

Joran frowned and looked up. Sure enough, a dragon ship hung in the air above the unseen fort. A little shiver ran up his spine. They wouldn't have come back before receiving Joran's message unless something serious had happened.

He hurried to climb down. Forcing his growing anxiety aside, Joran turned back to their guide. He still hadn't gotten the man's name. Or at least he hadn't gotten it spoken slowly enough that he learned the pronunciation.

"Thank you very much for your help. The introductions and traveling by sleigh saved us weeks." Joran held out his hand. "I hope I have a chance to return and visit your land again."

Their guide grasped his hand in the imperial style rather than his wrist as was done here. "You will be welcome, Joran. Have a safe journey home."

The man spoke with deliberate slowness to allow Joran to understand his words. Despite their time together, Joran still couldn't figure out how they spoke so fast and all at the same time yet still perfectly understood each other. He suspected there was magic involved, but saw nothing when he looked through the ether.

The second sleigh had joined them and Stoneheart and Grub climbed out. After a few brief words of goodbye, their guides were on the move again, this time back to their village. The visit had been brief, but Joran found he both liked and respected these people more than any other he'd visited so far. Their open honesty was a balm to his cynical soul.

"Why's our dragon ship here?" Stoneheart asked.

"I don't know, but I'm eager to find out." Joran set out for the fort at a brisk walk. The snow was slippery enough to make anything faster iffy.

Part of him, the part that worried about Alexandra, wanted to run. Lucky for him, the prudent part pointed out that she was likely safer at the palace than he was in the middle of nowhere. The One God above, he hoped that was the truth.

Half an hour later they reached the fort and found the gate open and Ramirus waiting in the courtyard. He wore enough clothes to make you think he planned a visit to the top of the highest mountain. What interested Joran was the scroll clutched in his trembling right hand.

"Message, Lord Den Cade," he said.

Throat tight and mouth so dry he couldn't speak, Joran accepted the scroll and unrolled it. Mia edged closer and read along with him. A wizard had attacked the palace in Tiber. Alexandra and her family escaped and were safe, or at least as safe as possible under the circumstances. They planned to stop at the Fourth Legion barracks before moving on to the church fortress. She wanted him to meet her at one or the other as quickly as possible.

"Signal the dragon ship, Commander," Joran said. "We're leaving."

"Bad news, my lord?"

"Exceedingly bad. Despite the cold, you should thank your lucky star that you were posted here—it may well have saved your life."

Ramirus barked an order and a legionnaire nearby waved a large red flag. A moment later the gondola started to descend.

He touched his fist to his heart. "Safe journey, Lord Den Cade."

"Thank you, Ramirus. And take heart, spring isn't that far away."

"You've clearly never spent time in the mountains. The cherry trees will be blossoming in Tiber while we still have a foot of snow."

Joran grinned, clapped him on the shoulder, and strode toward the gondola. A single crewman opened the door for him. A minute later they were all inside and on their way up. Calming his racing mind proved impossible until Mia touched his back. Peace flooded through him and he let out a long breath.

"I know she's safe, or was when she wrote the letter, but I won't really believe it until I see her with my own eyes."

"Have faith," Mia said. "This is the Iron Princess we're talking about."

He nodded. Joran appreciated her trying to cheer him up, but they both knew that the Iron Princess was in large measure an act. Not that he would ever underestimate Alexandra, especially if she had an army to command. But they'd learned to their detriment that when magic was involved, you couldn't count on anything.

As soon as the gondola locked in place, Joran went straight to the bridge. Everyone stood at rigid attention when he arrived. The captain might not know what the scroll said, but he knew it had to be serious.

"Orders, my lord?"

"We're going to the east coast. Make a long loop well to the north of Tiber. I begrudge the time, but we can't risk getting close."

"Beg pardon, my lord, but that area is sealed by the church. No one is allowed to pass whether on foot or by dragon ship."

"Unless they have some way of stopping us, that's the way we're going. Assuming you don't want to take our chances with a wizard powerful enough to drive off the First and Second legions."

The captain's throat worked as he tried to swallow. No one wanted to get on the wrong side of the church, but getting blasted out of the sky would be far worse. Especially since it meant he wouldn't be able to help Alexandra.

"If anyone complains, I'll take full responsibility. You're just following orders. Fair enough?"

"As you command, my lord." He shouted an order down the speaking tube and seconds later they were moving.

"We'll be in our cabin. If anything out of the ordinary happens, come get me at once." Joran didn't wait for a reply as he strode out of the bridge.

As soon as they were out of earshot Mia asked, "What do you think the church wants to hide?"

"I have no idea and right now I don't especially care. All that matters is getting to Alexandra in one piece." Joran frowned when a thought occurred to him. "Didn't Rufious say that Samaritan went northeast when he tried to find the Prophet's homeland? I wonder if that's what they're hiding. You just know a past pope had to have sent a team to investigate the fraud."

"That would certainly explain why the church doesn't want anyone exploring the area. Then again, from what I've seen, it's well within the realm of possibility that there's something horrible and evil in the area that they're keeping secret."

Joran set his kit on the floor and flopped into his hammock. "They do like their secrets. I'm going to try and rest. It's been a long few days."

Mia nodded and settled in one of the room's two chairs.

Joran closed his eyes, but couldn't stop thinking about what waited for them. Whatever they found, he doubted it would be pleasant.

CHAPTER 24

Khashair sat in a dark corner of his armory and stared at nothing in particular. Since failing to kill the emperor and pope, he'd been stricken by overwhelming depression. He recognized it as coming from Samaritan, yet even knowing that, he couldn't force himself to act. When they returned, he barely found the will to order his soldiers to train above ground so they wouldn't see him like this. If they did, magical binding or not, he might lose them.

Despite fighting with every ounce of will he could muster, Khashair still failed to overcome Samaritan. It was impossible, intolerable, yet no less true.

You said you'd destroy the empire and kill the ones that betrayed me. You said you had the power to grant me my revenge. And what did you accomplish? You killed a bunch of guards and soldiers that will be replaced in a year.

Khashair's mind raced. Samaritan's consciousness had finally made contact. He needed to snap him out of this funk now, before he vanished back into the recesses of his mind.

"What about your friend? The one in Dwarfhome. Are we

just going to sit here in the dark while he languishes in that cell?"

Titus. He must be freed.

"He will be, if you help me. You need to shake off your mood. Let me do what needs doing."

Khashair waited, forcing himself not to hold his breath.

Slowly the fog of depression lifted and soon steely determination replaced it. Thank heaven. He sprang to his feet and hurried outside. The cultists were standing in neat lines swinging swords and giving a credible impression of being soldiers. From the length of the shadows, he guessed noon had passed not that long ago. Perfect, they should be fed and ready to fight.

"My friends!" he said. When everyone had stopped their practice and turned to look at him, he continued. "I have completed my preparations. The time has come to make our next strike on the corrupt empire. The wealthiest province will feel our wrath. Ready yourselves, we go to Dwarfhome."

They didn't cheer. The magical alterations his potion had made rendered them incapable of powerful emotions. Instead, they hastened to strap on their black armor. In minutes, his little army stood at attention, ready to march once more into battle.

He offered a thin smile and reached for the bile running under this tower. The smile vanished when he found less than he expected. The flow of bile rose and fell from time to time, but this felt different.

Titus is waiting.

He shook off his hesitation. There was plenty for what he needed and Khashair didn't dare delay lest he lose his unpredictable partner to a second bout of depression.

A portal opened at his command and the soldiers surged through ahead of him. An instant later Khashair appeared in a massive cavern filled with stone buildings. To his right waited a walled compound where they'd seen Titus and to his left was the bulk of the city.

A shout went up and a century of dwarves in heavy armor and carrying axes came charging toward them. The numbers were about equal, but black iron weapons were far stronger than steel ones.

Khashair left them to fight and made his way toward the walled compound. Crossbow bolts clattered off his shield as he drew closer. Twenty guards stood outside in front of the portcullis, shields locked.

He shook his head and pointed.

A bile-enhanced fireball shot out.

The explosion sent bodies flying in every direction.

With the path clear, he pointed again, this time at the iron bars blocking his way. They glowed red then blue then finally white before melting into puddles of slag.

He stepped through and glanced left and right. There had to be more guards than the twenty out front.

With a shrug, Khashair strode toward the larger building. Magic crashed into the heavy iron door, blowing it inward and reducing it to a twisted mass of scrap.

No soldiers waited on the other side. In fact, the entry hall held nothing save a few blocky decorations. Where the hell was everyone?

Titus is on the second floor.

Right, best rescue the unlucky fool before Samaritan decided to do something unwise like try and take over his body.

A set of stairs waited not far from the entrance and he climbed them. Reaching out with his magic, he sensed only one life force. Curious now, he pressed the spell out further and confirmed that there was only one person in the entire building.

Khashair clenched his fist. They'd been warned. That's why

everyone of any importance was missing. They were hiding from him. He buried his rage at the delay Samaritan caused and hurried toward the person he sensed.

Just as he'd hoped, he soon found himself standing in front of the same door he'd seen during his earlier scouting run. The man inside lying on the bed looked to be in good shape; no signs of abuse or torture were visible.

Of course not. The Den Cade family is an important one. The governor wouldn't do anything that might offend them.

"Would they not be offended by having a member of the family locked up?"

Not if another member asked them to do it.

Khashair placed a hand on the door and blasted it to ash.

Titus sat up and stared for a moment then said, "Bellator? How…? What happened?"

"That is a long story. The important thing is that I'm here to get you to safety. Follow me."

Titus didn't move. "Are you okay? You sound different."

Let me talk to him, just for a moment.

Khashair checked again, but there was still no one in the building. It seemed the cowards didn't even plan on trying to fight him. He had to give them credit for intelligence at least.

He let his psychic presence fall back just enough to allow Samaritan to control his mouth.

"It's alright, Titus. A lot has happened since we parted ways, but the plan is moving forward. Please, come with me. I need to know you're safe so I can move forward and create the world we dreamed of."

Titus finally relaxed. "I'm glad you're okay. I feared Joran might have captured you too. Where are we going?"

Khashair surged back to resume control. "Somewhere you'll be safe until the fighting is finished. Let's go."

Before the pair could take a step toward the stairs, a tremendous explosion shook the building. A shiver, for lack of a better word, ran through the ether. Someone had just cast a very powerful spell. Only the vampire had strength enough for something like that.

She would soon regret her arrogance in coming to face him.

CHAPTER 25

Fane tapped her fingers on the control panel and waited. It felt like she'd been waiting for a long time, though it certainly hadn't been more than a few hours. Given the amount of Black Bile that needed to drain, that wasn't really so long. But now that she was this close to the end, she wanted to get on with it.

Another half an hour passed and finally one of the runes burst to life. She checked her notes on the floor and nodded once. That confirmed it. All the bile had been sent to the lagoons. Now to make sure no one could undo her work.

Fane walked over to the door and looked out of the gash she'd cut in it. Beastmaster sat in a chair made from the severed limbs of the golems he'd destroyed. She shook her head. Sometimes it really was hard to remember he wasn't an actual twelve-year-old child.

"I need the sword."

He hopped down and ambled over, offering her the Hell-forged sword hilt first. "Are you finally done?"

"Yes. One thing remains then I'm going to hunt Khashair down and kill him."

"What about Samaritan?" Beastmaster sounded more curious than concerned about their one-time ally's fate.

"What about him? He chose to stand with our enemy. I won't countenance such a betrayal. And even if I was willing to overlook it, I doubt I could kill Khashair without destroying Samaritan's body."

She took the sword over to the control panel and slashed once, top to bottom and left to right, cutting a deep groove through the surface and sending sparks shooting through the ether. A second slash in the opposite direction completed an X three inches deep. No ether flowed through the panel and the diagram above had gone dark.

Prefect, now no one could send bile through the pipes.

Fane's original plan had been to take control of the power, but now she preferred to keep it hidden away. Without that extra power, no one on this miserable world had a hope in hell of besting her. At least that was her default thought. When she confronted Khashair, the truth of her theory would quickly be proven. The idea that she might be defeated again didn't even enter her mind.

"So what now?" Beastmaster asked from outside.

She sheathed her sword, turned into mist, and flew out into the hall to solidify. "Now we find Khashair and I kill him."

Beastmaster nodded. "Anything you want me to do?"

"Yes. Go to my citadel and prepare a portal. Should I need to escape in a hurry, I want you ready to open it."

His youthful face crinkled up in confusion. "You want *me* to go to your citadel? All the defenses are active, right? I don't want to have to blast through all your servants to get to your casting chamber."

Fane grimaced. "The command to bypass the wards and guardians is 'welcome the king of darkness'. Do not take advantage of my trust. If I find anything out of place when I get back, I'll strangle you with my bare hands."

"How long have we been working together?" He cocked his head. "Do you really think the threats are necessary at this point?"

"Maybe, maybe not, but they make me feel better. Contact me when you've completed the ritual preparation. I'll concentrate on finding Khashair."

"Okay, good luck. Not that you need it." Beastmaster became one with the ether and vanished.

Good luck, huh? Though she'd never admit this to Beastmaster, right now she wouldn't turn down a little good luck.

———

F ane usually needed a solid hour to prepare the portal ritual so she figured Beastmaster would need at least twice that long. Annoying as the wait was, she still needed to find Khashair. If she failed at that, nothing else mattered.

A focus made scrying easier, so she used the ether to polish her Hell-forged sword until it shone like a mirror. Staring into it, she gathered power and pictured Khashair. Samaritan's familiar face appeared in her mind's eye and she projected it into the ether.

The magic reacted at once. Her psychic form shot at the speed of light northwest and then underground. She pulled up short and looked around.

He was in Dwarfhome?

Why would Khashair come here? It was a province. A rich one to be sure, but hardly as important as the imperial homeland.

He must have a reason. Whatever it was, Fane didn't care. As long as she knew where to find him, nothing else mattered.

Movement below caught her eye. Black-clad swordsmen were battling dwarven legionnaires. And getting the best of it from what she could see. A closer look made it clear that the swordsmen weren't ordinary humans. Something had been done to make them stronger. Their bodies emitted a faint ethereal glow.

They had to be her stolen cultists. If Khashair had meddled with them magically, there was no chance she could reclaim them. Better to destroy the lot and start fresh. It was a waste of time and resources, but she had plenty of both.

Now, where was Khashair himself?

As soon as she thought it, the ether obliged, pulling her toward the city center and from there into a walled compound she assumed was the governor's residence. There seemed far too few people around. Not that it mattered. Collateral damage had never concerned her and it certainly didn't now.

She finally found Khashair standing in a doorway on the second floor talking to a man she didn't recognize.

With nothing better to do until she heard from Beastmaster, Fane adjusted her spell to allow her to listen in on their conversation.

"A lot has happened since we parted ways, but the plan is moving forward. Please, come with me. I need to know you're safe so I can move forward and create the world we dreamed of."

That wasn't Khashair. Fane recognized the tone and inflections. Samaritan had taken control, at least for the moment. Only powerful willpower would allow him to seize his body back. Whoever that man was, he had to be important to Samaritan.

That could be useful.

Fane? Are you there? The ritual is complete. Just let me know when to open the portal and I'll do so at your position.

Finally.

Well done, Beastmaster. I'll begin my attack momentarily.

After a brief internal debate, she decided that fighting in the close confines of the governor's residence didn't suit her. Better to draw Khashair out into the main cavern where her enhanced physical abilities would give her an advantage.

Fane sent her psychic form to where her former cultists were fighting, and summoned her body. Body and spirit fused and a moment later she loosed a huge fireball that sent the cultists and more than a few dwarves flying in every direction.

That should draw the arrogant bastard's attention.

Keeping most of her attention on the governor's compound, she pointed at a still-standing clump of cultists and blasted them with lightning.

The magic ripped their bodies apart.

Another pair charged, their black swords raised.

Fane bared her fangs and drew her Hell-forged blade. Undead speed and strength proved an overwhelming advantage.

Three swings sent blood and body parts flying.

She sensed it a second before Khashair and the man from inside came running toward her.

Khashair paused and raised his hand. The delicious look of horror on his face would make her smile for the rest of her eternal life.

Fane gathered power. She'd end Khashair with a single spell.

Before she could loose it, he vanished, leaving a dumbfounded man staring around him like a fish out of water.

She barely had a chance to savor the coward running from her for a change when the surviving cultists gathered their wits and charged.

Maybe she couldn't kill Khashair, but at least she could get rid of his soldiers.

Using ether to augment her already potent physical abilities, Fane hacked and slashed. Blood and limbs flew every which way. Even when she was human, Fane hadn't been troubled by death and now it fazed her no more than cold or darkness.

Five minutes of slaughter found her surrounded by black-clad corpses. The dwarven warriors had sensibly fled the scene without looking back. Killing dwarves didn't appeal to her at the moment, so she turned her attention to Samaritan's human friend.

She strode toward him, ready to paralyze the man at the first sign that he planned to run. Judging from the way he was trembling, he couldn't run if he wanted to. Fane stopped in front of him and when his gaze met hers, she seized control of his mind.

"Who are you?"

"Titus Den Cade."

"Why were you with Samaritan?"

"He's my friend. I've been trying to help him build the new world he dreamed of."

Fane nearly laughed. This fool actually believed the nonsense they'd made up to bring converts into the cult. Samaritan must have really fed him a heap of fiction. Still, if they were friends and their bond was strong enough to let Samaritan take even brief control of his body, he might be worth keeping around.

"I'm going to take you somewhere for safekeeping. There may come a time when you can help me save Samaritan from his own mistakes."

"He's my best friend. Anything I can do to help him, I'll happily do."

What a good friend. Certainly a better one than a nihilistic, revenge-happy psychopath like Samaritan deserved. Not that she was one to talk. Fane hadn't had a true friend since she was a child.

Beastmaster, open the portal and link me to your tunnels. Once you finish, meet me there.

Okay. Just so you know, we're nearly out of Black Bile. I think there's only four vials left in storage.

For now, it doesn't matter. Just open the portal.

Half a minute later a swirling disk of ether appeared. They

stepped through and into the roughhewn tunnels that Beastmaster called home.

"Follow me."

Titus could no more disobey her orders than he could fly. They walked through the dark passage by a light she conjured for his benefit. Soon enough they reached the flesh pits. The White Knight should be pleased to get some company.

They reached the pit and she lowered him in with an ethereal rope. Shoving him would've been much more satisfying, but she hadn't saved him to risk breaking his neck now.

"What's going on?" the White Knight asked. His beard had grown long and scraggly during his captivity and the less said about his stink, the better. He made Fane glad she no longer had to breathe.

Ignoring his question, she turned to find Beastmaster marching toward her. His pale skin and bloodshot eyes spoke volumes about how much casting the portal had taken out of him. A little encouragement wouldn't hurt anything.

"The portal worked flawlessly, well done."

His eyes narrowed. "You never say anything nice to me. What are you up to?"

"Nothing, I swear. I just thought a compliment was in order given all you've done to help me over the past month."

He still looked suspicious, but his gaze shifted to the pit. "Another human. Are you collecting them now?"

"Hardly. This one is also friends with Samaritan. Close enough that he took control of his body away from Khashair. He may be useful during the final confrontation."

"I thought this was supposed to be the final confrontation."

"It would've been if he hadn't fled the instant he realized his power advantage was gone. Now I need to hunt him down again."

"Are you going back to your citadel?"

"To search. I'll return here in case I want to grab the humans before I attack. I do have another job for you."

Beastmaster grimaced and scrubbed a hand across his face. "Okay, but I need food and sleep first."

"That's fine. I have no idea how long it will take me to find Khashair. When you're ready, I need you to secure us a fresh supply of bile. Even I can't open full-sized portals without it. I'm returning to my citadel now. The crystal ball there suits me better than yours."

"Where am I supposed to get the bile if you drained all the springs?"

"The Black Iron Empire. From your description, the network of pipes was exposed when the dragon attacked. You can trace them to one of the lagoons and collect all you can carry."

"You give me all the nasty jobs."

Fane bared her fangs. "Would you rather go toe-to-toe with Khashair?"

"Fair point. I need half a day to rest then I'll head out."

Fane nodded. She hadn't the slightest idea where Khashair might have run, but she feared finding him a second time wouldn't be simple.

CHAPTER 26

The flight felt interminable to Joran, but he did his best to keep his emotions under control, more for Mia's sake than his. Since he really had nothing to do, he and Grub had resumed their magic lessons while Mia and Stoneheart took up sparring.

Joran felt bad for the centurion. Game though he was, Stoneheart really had no hope of beating Mia. Joran asked once why he bothered and Stoneheart said even if he never beat Mia, he did learn a lot and that those lessons might make the difference between living and dying in a real fight. Mia told him something similar about learning her own tendencies and weaknesses.

As long as it helped, nothing else mattered. Besides, the two of them seemed to be having a ball.

"You're not focusing, Lord Den Cade," Grub said.

Joran blinked a few times and looked at his teacher. Grub wore his usual brown robe and the two of them sat across from each other on the floor of the hold. Joran was supposed to be learning how to extend his sight from his body, but so far he hadn't had any luck. The fact that his mind constantly drifted didn't help.

He had to get his head on straight or he'd be wasting both his and Grub's time. "Sorry. I have a great deal to think about. Walk me through it again."

"Draw the ether into your eyes then picture a pair of phantom eyes coming out attached to your real ones by threads of ether. Focus on what you want and the ether will do the rest, assuming you can channel enough power."

"And if I can't?"

"Then the spell will fizzle. But don't worry about that. I've already seen you channel more than enough ether to activate the spell. It's your concentration that's the problem now. Sometimes the hardest part of being a wizard is putting aside everything else in your life and thinking only about the spell. That can take years and some wizards never master it."

"Really?" Joran leaned back and worked the kinks out of his neck. "How did they become real wizards if they failed that task?"

Grub's smile didn't reach his eyes. "They became fair-weather wizards. Perfectly useful when life was good and a mess when they had family troubles. I wouldn't want any of them with me in combat, but if you needed a vein of ore found or a tunnel checked for toxic gas, most of the time they were perfect."

Fair-weather wizards. Sounded like an insult and judging from the look on his face, Grub meant it that way and also as a challenge. Basically, what sort of wizard did Joran want to be, a reliable one or one that was only worth a damn when everything in his life was perfect? Given who he was marrying and what his life looked like at the moment, his life was never going to be perfect.

He'd just have to buckle down. It was no different than when he had a big project in the lab.

The sound of approaching footsteps broke the tense atmosphere. A crewman stepped into the hold and hurried over to Joran. "Lord Den Cade, the captain requests your presence on the bridge. There's something he thinks you need to see."

Given the young man's tone, it sounded serious, but since no one had sounded the alarm, not immediately dangerous.

Joran pushed himself to his feet as Mia and Stoneheart ended their match. "Let's go."

They quick-marched up to the bridge. Joran's breath caught in his throat when he looked out the front window. Buildings of dark stone dotted a valley surrounded by mountains. A strange black fog filled the area, drifting between the buildings, and generally making the village or whatever it was look inhospitable.

But what really drew his eye was the only place the fog didn't approach. At the edge of the village in the center of the clear area stood a hoop of silvery metal that immediately made him think of Mia's sword. Strange symbols unlike anything Joran had ever seen covered the surface of the hoop. The size of the thing impressed him the most. It had to be forty feet in diameter and weigh scores of tons. He couldn't begin to imagine how men might build such a thing.

"The One God be merciful," Mia said. "What is this?"

Joran's eyes widened when he finally understood. "This is what Samaritan was looking for when he set out on his quest. I'd wager every coin in the family treasury that the Prophet originally came from here. This is what the church wanted to hide."

"But why?" Mia asked. "What difference does it make where he came from? That doesn't make him any less who he is, does it?"

Joran shook his head. "I don't know. The pope said one of his predecessors sent a team to explore the area. Maybe they found something that would make a lie of everything the church taught."

He didn't add that everything they taught actually was a lie, so proving it shouldn't be that hard. The wrong person hearing that bit of information could cause them some serious trouble.

"What's that metal thing?" Stoneheart asked.

"No clue." Joran peered through the ether and found the construct empty of ethereal energy. Even if it wasn't charged with magic, it did seem to keep whatever that fog was well away. Just like Mia's sword and Samaritan's amulet did with the corruption in the Black Iron Empire.

"What should we do, Lord Den Cade?" the captain asked.

Joran really wanted to explore down there, but now wasn't the time. "Keep going, but make a note of this place on your charts. We're going to be coming back."

The stern-faced woman at the navigation station jotted something down. Just in case she was a true believer, Joran made his own mental notes of the local topography. If he had to, he could probably find this place again on his own.

The dragon ship slowly soared away from the shadowy valley. Joran didn't take his eyes off it until the mithril—and he was certain the giant hoop was the same metal as Mia's sword—moved out of sight. Joran couldn't say why he thought it, perhaps some intuitive leap brought on by his soul bond, but he felt certain they'd find the answers they needed down there.

CHAPTER 27

Antius scratched his filthy beard and wished for the he knew not how manyith time for a tub of hot water and a razor. If his fellow knights saw him in this state, they'd banish him from the order. He didn't even know how long he'd been rotting in this hole, though horrible as it was, he preferred it to the cold, wet, underground city where he'd left the bodies of the pope's mercenaries.

His gaze shifted to the still-groggy man his female captor had deposited in his cell. He looked familiar, though Antius couldn't place exactly where he knew him from. He was an imperial noble and a wealthy one from his fine silk clothes.

Like any good White Knight, Antius knew nothing about magic beyond needing to kill anyone he found using it. But he could tell that the woman had done something to affect the new arrival's mind. What, exactly, remained to be seen.

The man groaned and looked up at Antius. His eyes had lost the glassy look from earlier, but still didn't seem totally clear. "How did I get here? And where is here anyway?"

"One of my captors, a female wizard of some skill, dropped you in here. As to where we are, that is harder to describe. I am

Knight Commander Antius of His Holiness's White Knights. Who have I the pleasure of addressing?"

"Titus." He put a hand to his head and groaned again. "Titus Den Cade. The last thing I remember was looking into that woman's eyes. They glowed red. What sort of person has glowing red eyes?"

"An evil one. You would be Joran's kin?"

That perked him up a bit. "You know my brother?"

"Not well, but we fought a giant serpent together in Stello Province. He seemed a good man, if a bit less reverent than I liked."

Titus smiled, fondly Antius thought. "Yes, Joran is a good man, though somewhat misguided at times. Have we any hope of escape?"

Antius tapped the smooth stone of his prison wall. "Not unless you can climb this and defeat my other captor's mutated beasts. If you have any suggestions for getting out of here, I'm eager to hear them. Nothing has come to me and I've been here for weeks if not months."

Titus held his head in his hands. "I'm a merchant, not a soldier. If you want something appraised, I'm your man. Plotting escapes is a little outside my area of expertise. What do they want from us?"

"I haven't the slightest idea. I'm not even certain that they know what they want us for. The woman questioned me about one of my former comrades, an ex-White Knight named Bellator."

"You know Bellator?" Titus sat up straighter. "He freed me from a dwarven prison before fleeing the woman. He seemed... different. Not himself. In the years I've known him, he never acted like he did today. Perhaps she brought me here because we're friends."

Antius's eyes narrowed. If Titus was friends with Bellator now, he had to be mixed up in whatever insane plot Bellator was working on. Strangling him wouldn't be difficult and before his journey north with the mercenaries, Antius would have done just that without a second thought. But he'd learned too much, seen too much, to accept anything at face value.

"Did she ask you any questions?"

Titus nodded. "I think so. Everything that happened after I looked into her eyes is blurry. I don't remember what she wanted, only that she seemed obsessed with Bellator. I fear she may wish to use me against my friend."

"That is no doubt true. I suspect they have similar thoughts about me despite the fact that Bellator tried to kill me. He did at least look a little sad about it. Not that I would have been any less dead had that tree branch not broken my fall. That it almost broke my ribs seemed a small price to pay."

Titus looked up and for a moment Antius thought he might be praying. When he lowered his gaze their eyes locked. "Do you know what the church did to him?"

"I know some of it. He defied the pope and went looking for the Prophet's origin. A batch of mercenaries was dispatched to silence him. They failed. I volunteered to finish the job. He betrayed everything I believe in. And yet now I can't help wondering how much of what I believed is the truth."

"Would you like to know? I can tell you everything he told me. Whether you choose to believe it or not is up to you."

"Please do. I respected Bellator more than any man I had ever met. I have to know what made him betray all that he held dear."

"Then I will begin with the simplest and hardest truth that he shared with me. The One God is a lie. The man you call the Prophet was an insane, but still genius alchemist. He made up The One God and the first pope and emperor played along to wring out all of his secrets."

Antius stared at Titus but saw nothing to indicate that the man had lost his mind and he certainly seemed to believe what he said. That didn't mean he was right, but if Bellator found something that made him think that everything he'd been taught to honor was a lie and you combined that with the loss of his soulmate, it would certainly be enough to send anyone over the edge.

"You accept his heresy at face value?"

"Bellator has never lied to me. And when I told my brother, he confirmed that he knew it was a lie." Titus laughed. "Do you know what Joran said next? He said it doesn't matter if The One God is a lie. The people need something to believe in. A unifying faith. If the church hadn't made up The One God, someone else would have. It's simply too valuable an idea."

The more he heard, the tighter Antius's chest grew. The truth of that last statement more than anything else struck him. Spreading the faith motivated so much that the empire did. People would accept things more readily if they thought God told them to than they would if a mere mortal did. The White Knights themselves drew power from their faith. Not magical power, but mental power, the will to do anything for the church.

And all of it for a lie.

The thought shocked him. When did he acknowledge the ultimate heresy as the truth? He didn't remember making a conscious decision. Everything that had happened built up his doubts. Titus's story just drove the final nail into the coffin of his faith.

"Your brother is right," Antius said. "For all its many faults, the empire is a net good for the world. The people's faith makes it better than it might otherwise be. Without The One God and the church, who can say what horrors the nobles might be willing to commit."

"You're making my argument for me. Rather than relying on a lie to temper the nobles' actions, why not get rid of them and everything else crushing ordinary people and replace it with something better? That's what Bellator is trying to do."

Antius gave a sad shake of his head. "I fear you might be a bit too idealistic. Bellator wants revenge. I saw the madness in his eyes before he sent me to my near death. If something good comes from that revenge, so much the better. But I don't believe for a moment that he cares. All that was good and honorable in him is dead."

"You're wrong, but there's nothing we can do about it one way or another from this pit."

Antius leaned back and rested his head against the smooth stone. Wasn't that the truth.

———

Khashair's heart raced as he panted for breath in the safety of his armory. His golems made no comment as he gathered himself. The shock soon wore off, but he still had trouble wrapping his mind around the truth.

The bile was gone.

As soon as he arrived, he'd checked the pipe running under his tower and found it as empty as the one under Dwarfhome. Somehow the vampire had found the control bunker, translated the overrunes, and figured out how to drain the pipes. Only an overmage or the automaton assigned to guard the bunker should know how to do that.

He needed to refill the pipes, but first he needed to clear his mind. The loss of the cultists and their weapons and armor stung, but there were always more men, fools stupid enough to trade their free will for power. He could rebuild from this, though it would set him back months.

YOU LEFT HIM BEHIND!

Khashair clutched his head. Samaritan's psychic voice had never felt this powerful.

You left Titus for the archbishop. She'll kill him.

"Better him than us." The pain grew. Clearly an honest answer wasn't the way to go. "Without the bile's power, I have no hope of defeating that woman in combat. You know I'm telling the truth. I also can't open a portal big enough for a person to pass through. If we'd stayed, we'd be as dead as your friend likely is. How is that a better result?"

It's not. It seems the archbishop is now on my revenge list.

"That's fine. I need her dead as well. There's no way I can rule the empire with someone as powerful as her running around causing trouble. But first we need to go to the bunker and refill the pipes. Once my full power is restored, we'll hunt down everyone that stands in the way and kill them."

The pain vanished and, in its place, came a rush of determination. He and Samaritan were on the same page now. Aligning their souls would provide at least some extra power. And that might be the difference between death and survival.

Where is the bunker?

"On the coast. We built it to connect the original empire with the colonies. It should've been hidden and defended. I don't know how she found it much less overcame the golems. The bloody things are immune to magic! Even a vampire shouldn't have been strong enough to defeat ten of them without magic."

Several deep breaths calmed him and he pictured the over-rune hidden in the control chamber. Combining that visualization with his teleportation spell would allow him to bypass the wards that prevented magical entry.

An instant later he stood in the dark chamber. A conjured light appeared at his command and he stared in horror at the control panel. Two deep grooves had been cut in the surface, shredding the magic and rendering it useless. The floor was covered in overrunes along with their Imperial translation. It must have taken her days to do all this.

Even worse, Khashair couldn't fix it. The destroyed rune board needed to be removed and a brand-new one put in its place. He'd need months to create one along with reference books in his library back in the empire, assuming it had even survived the dragon's rampage.

Why don't we just go wake the dragon like I planned? Let it destroy everything we hate.

"Because I have no desire to rule a dead continent. If I wanted to do that, I'd just return to the Black Iron Empire. No, we'll have to find another way to kill the vampire. And until we do, I'll be keeping to warded areas and sunlight."

Khashair preferred to be the hunter, but for now it seemed he was the prey.

CHAPTER 28

Joran's trip home was turning into a voyage of discovery. A day had passed since they left the dark valley behind and the dragon ship had turned back south toward the Fourth Legion's barracks. Below them, another remarkable sight had appeared, this one being a depression over a mile across and at least fifty yards deep. He recognized it at once from the pope's description of where they lost Samaritan the first time. In its own way, the pit was as remarkable as the mithril hoop.

Mia stood beside him on the bridge as they stared down at the sunken forest. Though she remained silent, Joran felt her awe through their link.

"The world really is a big place," she said at last.

Joran knew exactly how she felt. His world used to be little more than his lab and apartment. It had expanded considerably over the past year. For better or worse, he was never going back to his old life. He'd made peace with that when he accepted his future was with Mia and Alexandra.

"Is that a cave?" she asked.

Joran squinted and sent a little ether into his eyes, sharpening his sight. He'd learned this trick on his own while working to master the spell that extended his vision. Sure enough he spotted a dark opening in the cliff face. From the look of it, something was using the entrance fairly regularly. Whether man or beast he couldn't tell.

"Captain, hover above the cave. I want to take a closer look."

"Yes, my lord." He sounded like Joran had suggested he walk into a lion's den.

The dragon ship changed course, eventually stopping directly above the cave. Now to see how well he'd mastered his new spell.

A deep breath steadied his breathing and he adjusted the flow of ether in his eyes. Next, he created phantom eyes and connected them to the real ones. When his lids closed, he could still see perfectly.

So far so good.

Finally, he lengthened the connecting thread and sent his vision flying down toward the cave. The phantom eyes reached the entrance with no problem and he felt no strain from the spell. Now to see how far he could go.

He floated down a set of steps to a roughhewn tunnel. For some reason the phantom eyes had no trouble seeing in the dark, though everything was in shades of gray. The first tunnel led to a room with a chair in the middle. It looked like a half-assed attempt at a throne room. Two of the biggest weasels Joran had ever seen were sleeping beside it. They were the size of mastiffs.

He shook his head. Who in their right mind would keep something like those things around?

Leaving the throne room behind, he flew down another passage. The tunnel ran for quite a ways before finally opening into a larger cavern. This one was a bunch of pits bored into the floor. What sort of beasts lived in these?

He flew higher and looked down.

They were empty save for one that held a pair of men. Was this a prison of some sort?

His construct moved closer and Joran winced at the sudden pain in his head. He had just about reached his limit. Best wrap this up quickly.

Ten feet from the prisoners, the cleaner of the pair looked up.

Joran's jaw nearly hit the floor.

What was Titus doing here? He was supposed to be safe in a cell in Dwarfhome. If he ever got his hands on that useless excuse for a governor, Joran swore he'd wring the dwarf's neck.

The pressure grew too strong and he ended the spell.

The bridge appeared blurry for a moment before he got used to using his actual eyes again.

"Why is your brother here?" Mia asked.

"You saw?"

She nodded. "It was weird, like what you saw was laid over what I was actually seeing. It was starting to give me a headache."

"It certainly gave me one. Think you can kill two giant weasels? They were the only guards I saw."

"After demons, I can't imagine weasels of any size giving me much trouble. We're going to get him?"

"I can't leave Titus here. Whatever his crimes, he's still my brother."

Joran would've sworn he heard the captain sigh, but when he looked up the man wore his usual, stern expression. "Shall we descend low enough to deploy the gondola, my lord?"

"Please do. And just in case, order teams to the flame emitters. I expect no issues, but better to be ready."

The captain touched fist to heart and barked orders down the speaking tube. Joran led Mia off the bridge and to their room. He collected his kit. Mia always wore her sword, so she was ready. Once they'd rounded up Stoneheart and Grub, it was back to the hold. Luckily for them, a dragon ship carried plenty of spare rope. Grub got the duty of carrying a coil.

The gondola crew was in place when they arrived and one of the men opened the door for them. Several minutes later the dragon ship stopped and the captain's slightly garbled voice came through the tube. "In position."

"Lower us when you're ready," Joran said.

The clamps clanked free and they were on their way down. The descent took longer than usual and Joran explained what they were doing to the dwarves. To their credit, neither of them offered a word of complaint. Stoneheart just pulled his axe from its loop and nodded once.

For his part, Grub grinned and said, "Sounds like you've gotten the hang of the vision spell."

"My range isn't that great."

"You just need practice. Using magic isn't that different from building muscles. The more you do it, the stronger you get. Up to a point anyway."

The gondola rattled when they hit the ground. Stoneheart shoved the door open and they piled out. As soon as they were clear, it rose thirty feet, high enough to keep anyone from reaching it, but low enough to give them almost instant access should they need to escape in a hurry.

Mia drew her sword and took point. At the edge of the darkness, Joran conjured a white light to guide them leaving Grub free to cast should they run into trouble. Stoneheart brought up the rear as they descended.

Since she'd seen the tunnels as well, Mia made a beeline for the prison pits. The little group hurried through the tunnel, facing no opposition. Joran expected something to happen at any moment, but so far, his worries were for nothing.

A minute later they reached the large cavern and went straight to the pit holding Titus. Both men stared up at Joran, mouths slightly open and eyes wide.

"Are you two strong enough to climb?" he asked.

Titus scrambled to his feet and the other man joined him more slowly.

"How did you find us?" Titus asked.

"Dumb luck. We can go over the details later. Let's get you out of there."

Grub uncoiled the rope and tossed one end down. He and Stoneheart braced themselves as Titus started climbing.

Joran turned his attention to the other man. "My name is Joran Den Cade. Who might I have the pleasure of addressing?"

"If you don't recognize me after our hike through the jungle, I must be in worse shape than I thought."

"Antius?" Joran knew the knight commander's voice at once. Though it had certainly lost some of its stridency. "I imagine your story is even more interesting than my brother's."

Titus reached the top and Joran grabbed him under the armpit to help him out. As soon as he cleared the rim, Antius started up. He climbed hand over hand and, far faster than Joran expected, he was out as well.

Grub started to coil up the rope.

"Leave it," Joran said. "Let's get out of here before something nasty shows up."

A hiss drew his attention to the cavern entrance. The giant weasels he saw earlier were standing in the entrance.

Mia angled toward them, sword cocked and ready.

"Wait," Antius said. "Their fur is nearly impossible to cut. You need to stab them with all your weight behind it."

"I think you'll find Mia's sword cuts better than most," Joran said.

She'd closed half the distance between them when the weasels charged.

One leapt right at her throat.

Mia shifted left and slashed, cutting the weasel in half with a single blow.

The second beast loosed an earsplitting shriek and charged. Unlike its partner, this one went for her ankles.

Mia danced out of the way.

Her sword darted out.

The weasel lunged to one side, but still lost a paw.

It froze for an instant and that was all Mia needed.

She lopped its head off, flicked the blood off her sword, and sheathed it. "All clear."

"That's impossible." Antius stared at Mia and the dead weasels as if not believing what he saw. "It took everything my companions and I had to kill two of those things. She killed them as easily as I might a housefly. Beastmaster's going to be furious when he gets back."

"Then we'd best be somewhere else when he, whoever he is, arrives." Joran hustled everyone out of the cavern and back to the gondola.

Five minutes later they were safe on the dragon ship and on their way again. All he wanted was a nap, but talking to Antius and his brother wouldn't wait. They all gathered in the ship's galley. The crew took the hint and made themselves scarce after providing the former prisoners a hot meal.

Tears ran down Antius's face as he ate a rather stringy mutton stew. "Do you know how long it's been since I ate a decent meal? It seems a lifetime ago."

Titus seemed a good bit more ambivalent about his food. No doubt the lord governor had provided finer fare. Joran was content to wait until they completed their meal to exchange stories. He loved his brother, but Antius interested him more. The White Knight seemed like an entirely different person. What could have happened to make such a change in his personality?

With the last of the stew devoured, Joran said, "Who wants to go first?"

"I will," Antius said. "My story is rather boring. After parting ways in Cularo, I finally made it back to report Samaritan's identity to the pope. Eventually I joined a team of church mercenaries in hunting our fallen brother down."

"The church has mercenaries?" Mia asked.

"Are you really that surprised?" Joran countered.

"Good point. Sorry, please continue."

"We tracked him to this sunken forest where we encountered more of those weasels. They were created by a wizard named Beastmaster. He appears to be a subordinate of the woman that brought Titus from Dwarfhome. He tried to feed us to his other monsters. For some reason they decided to keep me alive. I assume my former friendship with Samaritan had something to do with it. I've been rotting in the hole for I know not how long."

"When did you set out?" Joran asked.

Antius frowned. "I'm not sure the exact date. Probably midfall."

"It's almost spring, so I'd say you were there for around three months."

Antius shook his head. "It felt like longer. A lifetime longer."

"I'll bet. When we get finished, I'll have the crew bring you hot water and a razor. If you don't mind a dragon ship crewman's uniform, cleans clothes shouldn't be an issue either."

"The One God bless you." Antius said the words, but they didn't hold the familiar conviction. Joran guessed he'd learned the truth.

"My turn, I suppose," Titus said. "I had been enjoying the hospitality of Dwarfhome's lord governor. A far nicer prison than my most recent accommodations I might add. Though the way that fat dwarf looked at me like I'd lost my mind was quite disconcerting. Anyway, one day not long ago there was a ruckus and servants came running past my room. No one said anything to me but soon enough it went deathly quiet in the fortress. The next thing I heard was Bellator outside my door. He sounded...different."

"Different how?" Joran asked.

"The way he spoke was off. His accent was wrong for someone raised in Tiber. He seemed like another person. Then something happened and he was Bellator again." Titus looked away and Joran suspected he was seeing Samaritan in his mind's eye. "Anyway, he freed me and said he'd take me somewhere safe. When we reached the courtyard there was a woman killing his followers. He raised his hand to do something magical and the look on his face..."

"What?" Joran asked.

"I've never seen such an expression of stark terror. The next thing I knew he was gone. Poof! Like smoke in a hurricane. The lady approached and I couldn't move. She looked into my eyes and everything went hazy. The next clear thought I had was when I found myself sharing a pit with Antius."

"She questioned me about Samaritan as well," Antius said. "My memory is also hazy. I don't know what magic she used, but it wasn't pleasant. I also overheard her saying that Samaritan had retaken control of his body from someone called Khashair. I assume that explains why his accent changed."

The idea that an unknown ghost, for lack of a better word, was using Samaritan's body was a bit of a stretch even for his imagination. Better to stick with more concrete facts for the moment.

"Do either of you have any idea where Samaritan is now?" Joran asked.

Antius shook his head.

"He disappeared with magic," Titus said. "From what he told me, I didn't think Bellator was that powerful. Maybe the other one—Khashair, did you say his name was?—used to be a wizard of some sort. I suppose he might be anywhere now."

"Yes, I fear he might be."

CHAPTER 29

Beastmaster appeared in a familiar clearing in the Black Iron Empire. His satchel was filled with empty vials. Now all he needed to do was find a bile source he could reach without killing himself. That sounded simple on the surface, but everything was so ruined here, finding an intact pipe would be no simple thing.

He smiled to himself and cast a flying spell. Fane always wanted him to take care of the nasty jobs. Not that she was wrong about him wanting to avoid a fight with Khashair. Even without the power boost, Beastmaster has serious doubts about his ability to beat the man one-on-one. If he could go into battle with all of his pets, that might be different.

No, it probably wouldn't be. His flyers weren't that strong and he felt certain Khashair would have no trouble taking to the air. Best to run Fane's errands and let her deal with the fighting. If he got lucky, maybe they'd kill each other and he could get back to researching in peace.

Fat chance of that.

He soared north, and soon reached the broken edge of the island. Now to find a pipe.

A hundred yards east he found a bent length of black iron that might well have been a pipe once jutting ten feet out of the cliff face. He sent a light down it and squinted. Looked like it was pinched shut about fifteen feet in.

Useless, not that he was surprised. Having already seen the state of the place, he knew this wouldn't be an easy task. He flew a complete circle around the island and found no more pipes.

Beastmaster considered his options as he floated over the island. He snapped his fingers. There had been bile filling that pit in the underground complex he'd found. That would be the perfect place to fill his vials, assuming it hadn't drained completely when Fane did whatever she did.

He zipped back to the clearing and found everything exactly the way he left it. Good, he didn't especially want to dillydally. Fane would want to move as soon as she located Khashair. He landed and made his way through the dark, empty tunnels to the bile pit.

He cursed the universe when he found it drained. Was it too much to ask for one thing to go right for him? Maybe the local lagoon wasn't too deep.

Extending his vision, Beastmaster sent his sight through the floor of the pit and along an empty pipe. It went straight down for far too long but finally ended at a lake of bile. Not ideal, but if he blasted the lid off the pipe, he should be able to send the vials down one at a time and fill them. "Should" being the operative word.

He shrugged. One way to find out.

Ether gathered at his mental command and took the shape of a crowbar. He jammed it under the seal. Or at least he tried to. As soon as his construct hit the black iron it shattered.

Looked like the cap was enchanted the same way the golems were. That wasn't exactly ideal.

He tapped his chin and looked around. They had to have a way to open and close the seal that didn't involve traveling across the ocean. Maybe he could even pump some of the bile to the top. That would save him all kinds of time.

Beastmaster peered through the ether looking for anything that might be an activation rune. While he still had no idea how to read the runes, at this point he would happily push any button he found on the off chance it worked.

Alas, it wasn't to be. A thorough search of the room revealed nothing that even resembled an activation rune. He scrubbed a hand across his face. Looked like he'd have to do this the hard way.

Returning to the pit, he conjured a pickax and slammed it into the stone beside the seal. The rock, at least, had the good grace to smash apart, leaving a decent-sized divot.

Time to make like a dwarf and dig.

———

K hashair considered the time and decided the sun should be all the way up in the empire. He needed to get more Black Bile and his best chance would be returning home. Even destroyed, he should have a better chance of finding something there than in the colonies. And the vampire would be less likely to show up as well.

He'd been pacing and thinking in his supply depot for he knew not how long. Days certainly. The loss of his biggest advantage had shaken him to the core. But he was over it now. He didn't become an overmage without facing obstacles and this was just one more that needed overcoming.

There was an intact workshop where we fought my enemies. Would there be a usable access there?

"Indeed. Those workshops were built directly over bile lagoons to make it easy to draw whatever quantity of power the wizards needed. I can even teleport to the clearing based on your memories. I just need to collect my bile flask."

What's that?

Khashair went to the alchemy supply cupboard and frowned at the empty slots. He'd wasted far too many potions on those almost certainly dead cultists. He shrugged and crouched to open the bottom doors. Inside was a black iron flask marked with overrunes. It was long and narrow with two straps that attached it to his forearm. He grabbed a larger, one-gallon reservoir as well.

"We used the flasks when we invaded a new territory. Since we hadn't extended the pipe network yet, it was necessary to carry a supply of bile with us. It's nowhere near as convenient, but it gets the job done." He straightened, attached the flask to his right forearm, and slung the reservoir's strap over his shoulder. "Never thought I'd have to use one of these again."

He glanced at the golems. It would've been nice to bring at least a few along with him, but he couldn't teleport with them and a portal was out of the question with only his personal power. No, if he ran into trouble, he'd need to get his own hands dirty.

Ready as he'd ever be, Khashair became one with the ether. An instant later he appeared in a clearing with a hole dug in it. The overcast sky and corrupted ether confirmed his location. Khashair hated it here. He hated the failure it represented. He and his fellow overmages had been so confident when they set out in search of the bile's source. The combined power of the overmages had been overwhelming.

He smiled at the bitter memory. They'd learned in a hurry what real, overwhelming power was when the dragon rose out of that lake of darkness. He shuddered at the memory. The others hadn't believed failure was a possibility, but he took nothing for granted. Which was why Khashair was here and they were ashes.

At the entrance to the complex, he frowned. A rhythmic pounding was coming from inside. Had some of the local demons moved in? That seemed unlikely since demons weren't known for their industriousness. At least in regards to anything not involving torture or murder.

Someone beat us here.

Not the vampire. Even with the clouds covering it, the sun was still up and she wouldn't be able to function even if she somehow survived the exposure. Though if she arrived last night and entered the workshop before sunrise, that would be another matter.

Only one way to be sure. Khashair extended his sight and sent it flying into the workshop.

Are you truly so scared of her?

"I haven't survived this long by taking unnecessary chances. Only a fool goes into battle when he's uncertain of victory."

In my experience, victory is only certain after you've won. Everything else is a crapshoot.

———

B eastmaster wasn't sure how long he'd been digging, but he was thoroughly sick of it. On the plus side, he did have a pretty good hole going. According to his spell, another six feet would get him to the lagoon—well, the cavern that held the lagoon anyway. From there it was just a matter of filling his vials and getting back home.

He wiped the sweat from his brow. Digging with magic tired you out nearly as much as using an actual tool. Some of his pets liked to dig, but none of them had strong enough claws to get through solid rock. He'd have to work on that, assuming Fane ever let him get back to his research. A rather large assumption at this point.

A shiver ran through the ether.

Beastmaster spun just in time to see an ethereal construct dissolve.

He let his own spell vanish and sprinted out of the chamber.

At the intersection he glanced toward the entrance. A single figure stood silhouetted by the sun.

He kept going.

There had to be another way out of here.

Of course, having explored the entire complex once already, he knew there wasn't. He was lying to himself to avoid panicking. There was only one person he could imagine coming here. Well, technically two, but Fane wouldn't show up in the middle of the day. That meant it had to be Khashair. No doubt he had the same plan as Fane.

Gather some more bile and go hunting.

Beastmaster reached the final chamber and found the small bile spring sealed with another of the magic-resistant black iron caps covering it.

Where should he try next?

He shook his head. There was nowhere else to try. Focusing himself, Beastmaster cast a message spell. "Khashair is at the underground workshop."

He pictured Fane and sent the spell rushing to her.

Not that she'd be able to get here in time to save him, but at least she'd know where to go to avenge him.

Assuming she bothered.

Footsteps were headed his way. Beastmaster clenched his fists. He refused to go down without a fight.

If he weakened Khashair enough, maybe Fane could finish him.

He sensed the magic a moment before a tiny portal opened. A vial of Black Bile emerged.

Thank the universe.

He snatched it out of the air, smashed the vial, and used the rush of power to loose a Dispel blast that blew the wards to bits.

Khashair stepped into the doorway a moment before Beast-master became one with the ether and vanished.

Beastmaster appeared, heart racing and body trembling, in his throne room. That had been far too close.

When the shaking subsided, he went to his scrying chamber. He'd expected his giant weasels to come running. Usually, they were eager for a pat on the head. Maybe they were hunting in the maze.

With a shrug, he waved a hand and a section of wall slid into the ground. He touched his crystal ball and pictured Fane. As soon as he did, he found his psychic form flying toward her citadel. When he arrived, he found her in a room similar to his though with a different style of crystal ball.

"You escaped," she said. "Congratulations."

"Thanks to you. I doubted you'd sacrifice one of our remaining vials of bile to rescue me."

"Your power is greater than the boost I'd get from one vial. It was an easy choice to make. I take it Khashair arrived before you secured us a new supply."

"Afraid so. I was close though. He can probably finish the tunnel I was digging in a few hours. If you hurry, you can kill him before he reaches the bile."

She shook her head. "I can't fight him in the Black Iron Empire. That's his home territory. Who knows what secret weapons he can call on? No, we need to stay on mission. Find an access point here and get us a new supply of bile. I'll keep an eye on Khashair."

"Sure," Beastmaster said. "Any idea where I should go?"

"You know where the bile springs are. Try one of them or all of them. I don't care, just get me what I need."

"I'll do my best."

He ended the spell and found himself back in his scrying chamber. Beastmaster didn't actually know where all the bile springs were. He usually got his supply directly from Fane. Given her mood, he decided it best not to point that out.

But he did have the atlas that laid out the pipe network. He could use that to find a likely spot. Before he went, he should check on the prisoners. Knowing Fane, she probably didn't leave them any food or water. It was lucky for her pets that they were all undead.

He made the short walk to the flesh pits and stopped dead in his tracks at the cavern entrance. Both of his giant weasels were lying on the floor. One had been cut in half and the other beheaded. While he might not be an expert at everything, Beast-master was an expert at flesh shaping. Nothing should have been able to do that to his pets.

Oh, no.

He raced to the prison pit and stared at the empty hole. A rope lay at the bottom, so at least he knew how they got out. But who took them and where did they go?

He hadn't the slightest idea. Bothering Fane again would only get him yelled at. Better to collect the bile and tell her when they met up face-to-face.

Yes, that would definitely be the way to go. He repeated the thought over and over in the hope that he'd eventually believe it.

———

K hashair could hardly believe it when the youthful wizard smashed the workshop's wards and vanished. Where had he gotten the vial of bile anyway? He hadn't sensed any when he approached.

Likely from the archbishop. She can open these little portals and send small objects through.

That made sense. The wards were designed to stop teleportation. Portals worked on a different magical theory. Well, he was gone and Khashair had work to do.

He went over to the sealed bile pit and touched the black iron plug. Ether flowed and he activated the manual override. The plug spun three full revolutions and flipped up out of the way. Unfortunately, while he could open the pit back up, the override didn't reactivate the flow. He'd have to dip the bile out of the lagoon below like some farmer's daughter at the village well. The image didn't please him, but then little that had happened recently did.

He conjured an ethereal rope and sent the flask down the pit.

What will you do after this?

"I'm going to hunt that vampire down and kill her. It's become perfectly clear to me that I have no hope of success while she lives."

She's probably at her citadel. I've only ever arrived by magic, but my memories might be enough to let you scry on her.

"We'll see. Now be quiet so I can concentrate."

The extraction process didn't actually take that long and half an hour after lowering the flask, he had a full flask and reservoir. If he had to use every drop of the stuff, he swore he'd finish the vampire once and for all.

"Show me the citadel."

An image appeared in Khashair's mind. Dark halls, shadowy rooms, a lingering presence of undead that stayed just out of sight. That wasn't much to go on. Given what he knew about the vampire, she would have powerful wards in place against both teleportation and scrying, portals as well if she was smart. And he had no doubt she was.

He needed to get back to his armory and fish out his crystal ball. Rushing in blind would be a terrible mistake. Once he had the lay of the land, a plan of action could be made. Only then would he make his move.

Deep inside, he knew this would be their final battle. One way or another, everything would be settled soon.

CHAPTER 30

"There it is, my lord," the dragon ship captain said.

Joran and Mia were standing together at the bridge window. His brother and Antius had been resting, save for when they ate their meals, for the past couple days. Antius he understood. The White Knight had been a captive far longer than Titus. Joran would've liked to spend at least a little time with his brother before they arrived, but he couldn't exactly blame Titus for keeping his distance. Joran had ordered him locked up after all.

He also had the dwarves keeping an eye on both of their guests. He didn't really think either of them would try anything, but with magic involved, Joran refused to take chances.

Shaking off his unpleasant thoughts, Joran focused on the sprawling compound below them. It wasn't as big as the palace, but the Fourth Legion's barracks was a huge military installation. There was a massive fortress, several acres for training yards, outbuildings, and a hangar big enough to allow the dragon ships to enter.

"I don't think I've ever been to a legion expeditionary fortress. Have you?"

Mia nodded. "Once. The princess brought me on an inspection with her a few weeks after she recruited me. I guess that was before I annoyed her so much."

He smiled and patted her back. Mia used to think she was in love with Alexandra, but now only lusted after her in a totally inappropriate fashion. It wasn't a huge improvement, but at least she no longer hovered over Alexandra like a worried lover.

"Should we go into the hangar, my lord?" the captain asked.

"No. Assuming Alexandra is here, I hope to make plans and be back in the air in a few hours. Collect whatever supplies you think you'll need and be ready."

"Yes, my lord." Again with the long-suffering tone.

Joran forbore comment and led Mia off the bridge. They'd collect the others and be ready to disembark as soon as the ship landed.

One level down they found Stoneheart leaning against the wall a little ways up the hall from the room Titus and Antius were sharing. Joran raised an eyebrow and got a head shake in return. So they hadn't left the room, good.

"We're almost there," Joran said. "Where's Grub?"

"In the crew quarters resting. His shift doesn't start for a few more hours. I'll grab him and meet you at the ramp."

"Thanks."

Joran took a few steps and knocked on the cabin door. Titus opened it a moment later. His eyes looked haunted when he peered out. Dark circles ringed them and his skin had a pale, unhealthy tone. He looked like a man on his way to his own execution. And depending on how Joran explained things to Alexandra, he just might be.

"Time to pay the piper I suppose," Titus said.

"That depends on you. Will you help us stop Samaritan? I know he's your friend, but even you must see what he's doing is wrong."

Titus smiled, but it looked exhausted. "It all seemed so

simple, so right, when he first contacted me. We've both seen the excesses and corruption of the nobles, and the church is little better. Smashing it all and starting fresh seemed like a good idea. Now I don't even know who my friend is. At the very least I'll do my best to stop whoever is controlling his body."

"Fair enough. I'll do my best to keep Alexandra from cutting your head off." Joran looked past Titus. "Antius. Are you ready?"

Shaved, washed, dressed in clean clothes with his pristine white cloak over them, Antius once again looked like the man they'd marched through the jungle with, albeit maybe a little thinner.

"I am. You saved my life, Joran. Until this is over, my sword is yours."

That sounded entirely too humble for the Antius he remembered, but perhaps that Antius died in the pit. Whatever the case, Joran wouldn't turn down any help he could get.

A little shudder ran through the hull. Joran had flown enough times to recognize the feeling of a landing. He led the way to the exit and found the crew putting the ramp in place and the dwarves waiting. Grub offered a nod but no word of greeting. He looked only a little less tired than Titus.

Well, they'd all be getting plenty of rest soon enough. Joran just hoped it wasn't the permanent rest of the grave.

The crewmen finished their work and moved out of the way. Joran led the way down and grinned when he spotted Alexandra emerging from the fortress. She had on regular soldier's fatigues and wore a sword belted at her waist. Even so, he'd seldom seen a more beautiful sight.

They met halfway between the fortress and the dragon ship. Alexandra leapt into his arms. Joran spun her around and kissed her before setting her back down. Much as he would've liked to linger, they really did have a lot to do.

"I missed you," she said.

"I missed you too. Sounds like you had a bit of an adventure."

She barked a laugh. "If you call fleeing the palace like rats before a terrier adventure, then yes, we had an adventure. Father, Rufious, and the pope are waiting in the staff meeting room. I suspect we have a great deal to discuss."

"What about your brother?"

She didn't look at him. "He's elsewhere. In case the worst happens, Father wanted one of us out of harm's way."

"A wise precaution." Joran waved Titus and Antius up. "Alexandra, this is my brother, Titus. And I'm sure you remember Knight Commander Antius."

She shot Titus a hard look, but he just bowed without comment. A wise decision on his part.

Turning her attention to Antius she said, "Knight Commander. You're looking a bit worse for wear."

"It's been a rough few months, Majesty. With your permission, I'll save my story until we're all together."

"Fair enough. Come on."

She led the way into the fortress. Joran barely glanced at the bare walls and stern legionnaires posted at regular intervals. His mind was running ahead of him, trying to figure out how to explain his theory in a way that made it sound like something more solid than an intuitive leap.

The answer came to him when Alexandra stopped in front of a closed door. The pope was here. He could confirm that the place they saw was the Prophet's home. It wouldn't be unreasonable to assume that important secrets might be hidden there. And unless someone else had a brilliant suggestion, they didn't have so many other options.

Alexandra shoved the doors open and they strode into a square room dominated by a round table surrounded by chairs and covered with a map of the empire. The emperor, pope, and cardinal all sat facing the door. Joran bowed and the others, save Alexandra, followed suit.

"We will hear your report," the emperor said. "And for The One God's sake I pray you have good news."

"I have news," Joran said. "How good it is, you will have to judge for yourself."

He took a breath and launched into a description of their journey since leaving the capital. There were murmurs of surprise when he described the Land of the Blood Drinkers. His conversation with the dragon drew louder mutters, but no one saw fit to interrupt.

When he got to the part about the mithril hoop Joran turned to the pope. "Does what I describe match what your scouts found when they sought the Prophet's origin?"

Septimus's scowl made his already unattractive face even uglier. "It does. We lost ten men on that mission. The survivors described... things living in the drifting darkness. It's a small wonder the Prophet was a madman. Anyone living in such a place would be."

"He lived there over five hundred years ago," Joran pointed out. "It might have been a far different place then. In any case, I think if we're to find a way to deal with both the wizard and our other enemies, we need to go there and look around. There may be secrets of alchemy that we can only dream of hidden somewhere in the ruin."

"It's a death trap," Septimus said. "If you go, you'll be throwing your life away."

"I appreciate your concern, Holiness, but if we do nothing, we're all liable to end up dead. I prefer to at least try and find a solution to our problems instead of waiting for the axe to fall." Joran looked at each of them in turn. "If there's an option I've missed, I'd love to hear about it. Dying unnecessarily, especially now that I have so much to live for, doesn't appeal to me in the least."

Only silence greeted his statement. They all knew the odds of finding a miraculous solution to their problems. Despite that, no one had a better suggestion. That spoke volumes about their situation.

Antius and Titus took their turns. To his credit, Titus made no effort to hide his involvement with the cult and Samaritan. From the look on the emperor's face, that may or may not have been a wise decision.

When they finished, Alexandra gave a more detailed account of what happened in the capital as well as the attack on Dwarfhome.

Joran scratched his chin. "It seems Samaritan, or whoever is using his body, is opposed to the vampire woman."

"The archbishop," Titus said. "Bellator described her to me though he made no mention that she was a vampire. She created and led the Cult of the One True God."

"Pointing out that you're joining a cult led by an undead would doubtless hurt recruitment," Septimus said. "Even the idiots she did convert would revolt should they learn the truth."

Titus opened his mouth, but Joran clamped a hand over his shoulder, hard. Whatever he was going to say got swallowed.

"Maybe we can wait and just let the two of them destroy one another," Rufious said.

"That would certainly be ideal," Joran said. "The problem is, more than likely one will survive then turn their attention back to us and we still won't have a way to deal with them. And even if our wildest dream does come true, what about the next magical threat? And there will be one. It's insane to imagine otherwise. We'll need a way to defeat whatever comes next."

"What's your plan?" the emperor asked.

"I wish I had a good one. The best I can come up with is me and my team go back and search for the Prophet's workshop or library or whatever. There's no way to make plans beyond that. We'll just have to deal with whatever we find when we arrive. Our dragon ship is still on standby taking on supplies. I hope to be back in the air in an hour or two at most."

"I'm going with you," Alexandra said.

"You most certainly are not," the emperor countered.

"I refuse to sit around here waiting for news again." Alexandra shot her father a glare. "The future of the empire will be decided on this mission. A member of the family needs to be there. Marcus is safe and with him the line of succession. What happens to me, in the grand scheme of things, is irrelevant."

"It is not irrelevant to me." The emperor's tone changed from ruler to worried father.

Joran remained silent. Nothing he said would change anything. If her father failed to convince Alexandra to stay behind, Joran had no hope of doing so. Much as he'd love to have her along, he couldn't deny that knowing she was safe would make his life a little easier.

"How many people are you thinking of taking?" Rufious asked.

That question earned him a glare from Alexandra.

"Just the ones that have been traveling with me. Mia, Stoneheart, Grub, Antius, and Titus. If we run into more creatures like the one that showed up at the palace, Mia's sword will be the only thing that can hurt it. The more people we have, the harder it'll be for her to protect them all and the more likely we'll be noticed."

Alexandra stabbed a finger at Titus. "Why would you bring that traitor along?"

His brother had the good grace to wince, but Joran refused to be goaded. "Titus and Samaritan are friends. It's clear that despite his current circumstances, some bond remains. My hope is that if he sees Titus, he might hesitate long enough for Mia to strike him down. I grant that it's a small, theoretical advantage, but at this point, I'm not willing to surrender anything, no matter how unlikely."

She frowned but didn't press her argument.

At the risk of getting yelled at Joran said, "If there's nothing else, I really do hope to get moving as soon as possible."

"I need to get some armor and we can leave," Alexandra said. She glared around the room as if daring anyone to tell her she couldn't go.

Joran looked around as well, but the emperor looked resigned and the pope indifferent. Well, his preferences and good sense be damned, it looked like she was coming along.

"I need to gather supplies from the alchemy lab. We'll meet up at the dragon ship. Okay?"

She nodded and stalked out of the room. Why was she so determined to join them? She was a fair hand with a sword, but Mia, Stoneheart, and Antius were certainly more experienced in actual combat.

Joran bowed to the emperor. "We'll do our best to keep her safe."

The emperor suddenly looked all of his sixty years. He blew out a long breath and said, "If it's a choice of saving Alexandra and saving the empire, choose the empire. There are too many lives at stake to do otherwise."

Joran wasn't sure he could follow that order, but he just nodded and turned toward the door. He had supplies to collect and a mission to complete that, The One God willing, wouldn't cost him the first woman he had ever really loved.

CHAPTER 31

Fane had lost track of how many days she'd been scrying virtually nonstop in her hunt for Khashair. Her only break came when she drained the life force from one of the prisoners in the dungeon—her last, more's the pity. Still, that meal would tide her over for a good week. At the rate she was going, she'd have to have Beastmaster fetch her a meal at some point. Her efforts to find Khashair had come to nothing. He was almost certainly holed up somewhere warded against scrying, just like Fane.

The stalemate couldn't last. Eventually one of them would have to risk leaving the protection of their wards. Since Fane had an immortal body and Khashair didn't, he should be the one to break first. Unfortunately for her, she lacked the patience to go with her immortality. If she hadn't found Khashair by the time Beastmaster contacted her, she'd make the first move.

She stood up and stretched. Her body didn't get stiff and she no longer felt true pain. The movement was more a memory of her time as a mortal. Her crystal ball needed a rest. Twenty hours of channeling ether through it was about all she dared risk. Shattering it would really slow her down.

Fane? I've got the bile. Where do you want it?

Finally.

"Bring it to my citadel then I'll open a portal so you can fetch the prisoners."

About that. They're gone.

"What!?"

Someone busted them out and killed my last two giant weasels. Those things really turned out to be a disappointment. They were cute though.

"Focus, Beastmaster. Where are the prisoners?"

No idea. There was a rope in the pit, but other than that nothing to hint at where they went. Does it really matter? I mean as far as secret weapons go, those two were dubious at best.

She swallowed a snarl. "Just bring me the bile. It's time we settled this once and for all."

Fane barely had a chance to cross her arms when Beastmaster appeared. Dirt covered his robe and his satchel bulged with filled vials. He held the satchel out to her. "Here you go. I filled them all."

She glared at him before snatching the satchel out of his hand. "Took you long enough."

"I had to do a lot of digging to reach a lagoon. Not to mention I had to fill them all one by one. I thought I made pretty good time. So what are we doing now?"

"We're going to lure Khashair here and kill him. When the sun sets, I'll go outside and lower the exterior wards. If he's paying attention, he'll see me."

"Yeah, but Khashair isn't an idiot. He's bound to know this is a trap. What makes you think he'll show up?"

"The same thing that's making me lower the wards. He has to want to settle things as badly as I do. Assuming he secured a supply of bile, he'll be overconfident and eager to finish me off. And when he does, I'll use his own power to destroy him."

"You think."

JAMES E WISHER

She stared at him a moment. "What?"

"I said, you think that's the way it's going to go. But you can't be sure."

"No, I suppose I can't. That's why I have you. Once we're fully engaged in battle, you will hit him from behind. Even a momentary lapse in his concentration will be all I need."

———

K hashair frowned at his scrying window. The sun had set about fifteen minutes ago and he finally felt a tug on his consciousness. As soon as he focused on it, he saw the vampire, her figure partly obscured by shifting, dark fog. She seemed to be standing in some kind of settlement, but it wasn't one of the Black Iron Empire's villages. The architecture was totally wrong. Not to mention there wasn't any damage from the dragon's attack.

He pulled back and widened his view. The frown deepened when he saw the mithril gate near the edge of the settlement. That, he could guarantee wasn't built by the empire. For one thing, there wasn't any naturally occurring mithril on this planet. Second, mithril was antithetical to the sort of corrupt magic the overmages specialized in.

Much as he'd like to figure out where the gate came from, the teleportation wards surrounding the village were of more pressing concern. To attack, he'd have to appear at the edge of the wards and approach on foot. That would leave him open to ambushes and traps.

She's calling you out. The archbishop wants a final showdown.

"That's insane. Even on her home turf and at night, she has no hope of defeating me now that I have a new supply of Black Bile."

Will you go to fight her?

Khashair hesitated. For all his bluster, he had to admit there

210

were risks, big ones. "I could wait until sunrise. She'll be helpless."

She will also likely be somewhere else. Somewhere you can't find her.

He was right, damn him. Fine. While Khashair disliked anything resembling a fair fight, this time it looked like he had no other choice.

Shifting his focus to the side of the village furthest from the mithril gate, Khashair forced the ether to mark a spot just outside the wards before ending his spell.

That done, he strapped the bile flask to his right forearm and slung the reservoir over his shoulder. With this much bile he could level the whole miserable village with power to spare.

"Golems, activate." His remaining black iron golems stepped out of their storage spots. Their eyes flashed red to indicate readiness and they stared at him waiting for orders. Seeing no reason to delay, Khashair opened a portal. "Advance."

The golems marched through single file and he followed behind. They appeared at the edge of the fog that hung in the village. A glance through the ether confirmed that it was charged with corruption. Hardly a surprise given that a vampire lived here. Well, corruption suited Khashair as well. The over-mages wielded it more often than they did pure ether.

Focusing on the majority of his golems Khashair said, "Spread out. Kill anything you find. Three of you will take up a defensive formation around me."

The golems clanked off into the fog. Most likely they'd encounter some sort of undead living in the empty village. He hadn't the least idea what they might find and doubted anything weaker than a true demon could harm them anyway. The remaining three took up position around him. One to his left, one to his right, and one behind him to watch for sneak attacks.

Ready as he'd ever be, Khashair strode into the fog.

F ane flashed a fierce smile at Beastmaster when she felt the ether crackle and a portal open. Khashair took the bait, just as she knew he would. Of course, he appeared where she expected, on the opposite side of the village from the portal. So much mithril would interfere with his bile-enhanced magic as much as it did hers.

She wore one of her Hell-forged swords on her back along with a bandolier loaded with vials filled with Black Bile. Combined with her innate abilities, she should have power enough to destroy an army, much less one arrogant wizard.

Her smile faded when she sensed a number of ethereal presences enter the fog. None of them were powerful enough to be Khashair. They also didn't feel alive. That meant more of the golems the overmages seemed so fond of.

"I'm going after Khashair," Fane said. "I want you to destroy the golems. Join me as soon as you're done."

"Sure, no problem." Beastmaster had the second Hell-forged sword clutched in both hands. An ethereal barrier surrounded him, blocking the negative effects of the fog. She'd already ordered her guardians not to attack him, so he should be free to move around the village without issue.

They split up and Fane put Beastmaster out of her mind. Whatever happened to him now wasn't her concern. Besides, having seen what he did to the golems at the control bunker, Fane had little doubt that he'd handle these with equal ease.

Fane turned into mist and flew silently through the village. In this from she was indistinguishable from the fog and would have no trouble sneaking right up to Khashair. Even better, she could sense every move he made as he strode through the fog. The arrogant fool probably didn't even realize it.

A minute later she spotted him. Khashair had a trio of golems with him and appeared alert. He wore a strange device on his right forearm and had a black iron container strapped to his back. That had to be his bile supply.

Destroy that and she'd have a huge advantage.

She solidified three buildings up, drew a vial, and squeezed.

The vial shattered and corrupt power flowed into her.

Fane stepped into Khashair's path and hurled black flames at him.

A casual gesture parted them like a boulder in a river.

She grimaced and vanished into the fog again.

"I thought you wanted a showdown!" he shouted.

Indeed she did, but on her terms, not his. Fane would keep up the hit-and-run tactics until she found some sort of magic that hurt him.

And once she did, there would be no mercy.

CHAPTER 32

"By The One God," Alexandra murmured from her spot in the dragon ship's bridge beside Joran. He knew how she felt. Hs reaction to seeing the massive mithril construct had been pretty much the same.

Below them the foggy village spread out like something out of a nightmare. Only a hundred-yard circle around the mithril hoop looked clear and normal. Joran wouldn't swear to it, but the fog appeared even thicker than he remembered. He peered through the ether and saw an occasional flash like a spell activating. Beyond that he could make out no details.

"Orders, Majesty?" the captain asked. He sounded a good deal less annoyed when Alexandra was onboard.

Alexandra shook her head and looked at Joran. "It's your mission. I'm just here to help."

Joran smiled but inside he was doing backflips. The whole flight he'd been dreading the unavoidable debate about who was leading the mission. If she was volunteering to defer to him, Joran had no intention of complaining.

"Hover near the mithril hoop. We'll descend there. As soon

as we're clear, put some distance between the village and your ship. I'll signal you with a flare when we're ready for pickup."

"Yes, my lord."

The dragon ship started to maneuver into position. Joran and Alexandra headed for the exit. Mia hopped up off the couch and fell in behind them. Joran still hated it when she had to follow along behind him. He figured if anyone deserved to walk at his side, Mia did. But given the narrowness of the hall, there really was no help for it. He couldn't exactly ask Alexandra to walk behind them.

After a brief stop to collect the rest of the team, they headed for the hold. The gondola crew was waiting for them and had the door open already. They piled in and a few seconds later began the descent.

Alexandra looked to Joran. "What's the plan?"

"All that corruption is liable to sicken if not kill anyone unlucky enough to get caught in it without magical protection. Grub and I will try and purify it before we begin the search."

Grub grabbed his arm. "How the hell are the two of us going to purify all that?"

Joran pointed at the mithril hoop. "I have a theory. Look at the fog. To me, it looks like a single, giant spell laid over the entire village. What do you think?"

Grub squinted for a moment then nodded. "Agreed. So what? That's still the biggest, most powerful spell I've ever seen."

"So I think if we can get it started, the mithril will draw the corruption in like a whirlpool. Or maybe imagine the fog as a sheet and the mithril hoop as a wringer pulling it in and squeezing the corruption out."

"That's great if it works, but what if it doesn't?" Grub asked.

"Then I'll come up with a plan B." Which might well be getting back in the gondola and running for their lives. He decided it best not to mention that possibility. Didn't exactly inspire confidence.

The gondola settled on the ground and everyone hurried to get out. As soon as they were clear, it rose back to the dragon ship. Joran ignored it and focused on the hoop. What was the best way to get the process started?

He glanced at Grub. "Suggestions?"

As the dwarf thought, the others, excluding Titus, formed a defensive perimeter. His brother crouched beside the hoop and did his best to stay out of the way. Alexandra had refused to let him have a sword despite Joran's assurances that his brother was a fair fighter. She really didn't trust him and Joran couldn't blame her given his past choices.

Finally Grub said, "I think we just have to grab a piece of the fog and try and pull it in. Watch what I do and copy me. The technique is simple; you just have to put all your will into it."

Joran nodded. He'd gotten good at putting all his will into the magic.

A crude hand made of ether formed in front of Grub. It shot out toward the fog and grabbed on. A rope formed next and it started pulling.

The fog bent toward them but not much.

Joran frowned. Even with the addition of his meager strength, it didn't look like it would be enough.

He glanced at the hoop. Maybe a little leverage would help.

Joran formed his ethereal rope and ran it around the hoop. As soon as the ether touched the mithril, it grew thicker and denser.

"Grub, look at this."

The dwarf grunted and turned his head. "By the stones! Hold on, let me reform my spell around that thing too."

A few seconds later a pair of hands easily twice as strong as the first one Grub made shot out to grab the fog.

It still tried to resist them, but this time when Joran pulled, the fog moved feet instead of inches. Yank by yank they drew the corruption toward the hoop.

Joran's head throbbed until he feared it might burst. From the look on his face, Grub was faring little better.

But neither of them yielded.

The longest five minutes of his life ended when the edge of the fog touched the mithril.

The pressure vanished as the silvery metal started to draw the corruption in. Just as Joran hoped, now that the process had started, it needed no effort from them to keep it going.

He happily slumped to the ground and rubbed his temples. With any luck, that would be the end of his spellcasting for a while.

"Are you okay?" Mia asked.

"Yeah, just tired. It'll probably take some time for the fog to fully clear."

"What should we do until then?" Alexandra asked.

"There's nothing we can do but wait."

———

The running part of Fane's hit-and-run strategy was working great so far. In her mist form, she blended in perfectly with the corrupt fog and as she expected, Khashair hadn't been able to find her. The hitting part, on the other hand, had been a monumental failure. Even her bile-enhanced spells hadn't gotten past his defenses.

She considered and immediately rejected a direct attack with her sword. There was no way she could kill him before that spell he used tore her apart.

So it was a standoff. But one that couldn't last. When the sun rose, she'd be forced to fall back to her citadel. Strong as the walls were, she held out little hope that they'd withstand his magic. Once the citadel fell, the sun would do the rest of his work for him.

As she drifted through the fog racking her brain for some

way to defeat him, something tugged at her. The pull grew gradually stronger and she found her mist form getting dragged toward the portal along with the fog.

What was going on?

Getting too close to that much mithril would be only a little less worse for her than the sun. With no other choice, she solidified on the roof of a flat-topped tower. From there she studied the magic and quickly ascertained the problem. The portal was sucking in the fog and purifying it.

But why?

It couldn't be Khashair's doing. They'd been playing tag on the far side of the settlement. Beastmaster was a couple hundred yards away hunting golems. Someone else must have arrived during the battle.

A faint vibration in the ether offered her only warning.

Fane leapt a moment before a blast struck the tower, blowing it to gravel.

Khashair stood ten yards away, hands raised, power gathering for another spell.

Fane snatched a vial from her bandolier and used the bile to power a raw destructive blast.

What it lacked in focus it made up in speed.

Not that it mattered. Khashair swept her attack aside as easily as he had everything else she sent his way.

"This is getting sad," he said. "Surely you can do better than hurling unrefined ether at me like an apprentice throwing a tantrum."

Fane grimaced, darted out of sight and kept running to put some distance between them. He was right, damn the man. Flailing about in the hopes that one of her spells got through his defenses wasn't going to work against such an experienced wizard. If Lord Sur saw her struggling like this, he'd laugh at her, or worse.

The image of her master's contempt galvanized Fane. She would find a way to defeat Khashair.

When she'd put half a dozen buildings between them, she stopped to think. She needed some way to take Khashair by surprise. As long as he could see her spells coming, he would have no trouble tearing them apart.

A slow smile spread across her face when the answer came to her. She just needed a few minutes to prepare.

K hashair could hardly believe he'd been so worried about the vampire. The woman had power certainly, and finding her using bile to increase it surprised him for a moment. But it didn't matter how much bile she used if she lacked the skill to fully control it. He and his predecessors had spent centuries perfecting the use of Black Bile in their magic. It was hardly a fair fight.

Not that such a thing interested him overly.

If you can beat her, then do so quickly. This fight is a distraction from my revenge. You promised me the pope's head and the life of every churchman.

"And you'll have them all. You've been waiting years for revenge. A little longer won't matter. Besides, if we can't eliminate the vampire, we'll be constantly looking over our shoulder. I don't know about you, but the prospect doesn't overly interest me."

Samaritan said no more and Khashair accepted that as acquiescence. Deep down, Khashair understood that he'd have no true peace until he granted Samaritan the revenge he so badly sought. Sometimes he wished he'd killed the man and waited to find a better host. But after centuries of waiting, any opportunity to escape was too good to pass up.

He stepped past the shattered tower and moved to follow his prey. She was fast and strong, but it really only helped her escape.

Now, where had she run to this time? Separating her darkness from the fog was the trickiest part of the hunt.

He frowned when he looked around. Something was happening with the fog. It was flowing toward the mithril hoop. It appeared someone had begun the process of purification. That suited him fine. Finding the vampire would be far easier without the fog confusing his senses.

"Khashair!"

He turned to see the vampire racing toward him, a black iron sword raised and ready in her hand.

Madness. A direct confrontation like this had no hope of reaching him.

He gathered magic and sent tendrils of corruption streaking out to tear her apart.

They struck hard, but landed on nothing but air.

He had just time enough to wonder what happened when a powerful blow struck his right side.

His personal shield stopped the edge from piercing his flesh, but the raw power behind the blow cracked his ribs and sent him flying down the street.

Khashair didn't stop until he slammed back first into another tower. The impact drove his bile reservoir into his back, nearly breaking his spine in the process.

Despite the pain, he scrambled to his feet, ready for the next pass.

He found the street empty.

Snarling in annoyance, he tried to sense her presence and found nothing. She must be suppressing her aura.

I warned you not to underestimate the archbishop.

"Shut up, shut up, shut up!"

He took a breath to calm himself. Anger would do him no

good.

Two of his golems stomped over to rejoin him. The third lay in two pieces on the ground. She'd cut through the golem and still struck him with that much force.

Unbelievable.

Alright, time to try something different. He moved to the center of the street, gathered power, and wove a spell circle with him in the center. Anything that passed through it would be instantly struck by his corruption-destroying spell.

Let's see the bitch get through that.

———

Invisible and with her power dispersed, Fane stood on the roof of an intact tower and stared down at Khashair. He was just standing in the street, a golem on either side. A magic circle surrounded him and while she couldn't tell exactly what it did, she doubted it would be anything healthy for her.

Was he hoping she'd be stupid enough to charge in without checking for traps? How insulting.

Still, she couldn't believe that blow hadn't cut him in half. Getting through the black iron golem must have taken just enough power off her swing to let him survive. One thing was certain, she didn't dare try that trick again.

Fane ground her teeth in frustration.

Activating a telepathy spell she said, "How goes the hunt, Beastmaster?"

I've cut down six of the golems so far. They seem to be wandering around looking for something to fight without any real plan.

"Keep doing what you're doing. When you've dealt with the last one, find me." She ended the spell.

Using Beastmaster as a distraction might work, but if she ordered him to do something suicidal, he'd refuse and having him turn on her was a very real possibility. If he joined

Khashair, she wouldn't have a chance. Beastmaster knew all her secrets. Or most of them anyway. Certainly he knew enough to make her life incredibly difficult if he changed sides.

Fane smiled to herself. It must be nice to have allies that were really loyal and not just serving out of fear. She wouldn't know.

She used a single thread of ether to pull a rock from the street to her hand. Let's see how his barrier handled the simplest of attacks.

Her arm shot forward, sending the rock speeding toward Khashair's head. It hit and bounced off, out of sight. The impact appeared to do no damage. Not that she had really expected it to.

"Is that the best you can do?" Khashair shouted. "Throwing rocks like a child?"

She ignored the insult. The rock had gotten through his spell circle, but not his personal shield. She could use that.

Another rock flew into her hand. This time she charged it with pure ether, forging a spell of mixed fire and lightning. Fane energized the rock until it nearly vibrated in her hand.

Let's see what this does.

The rock shot out even harder than the last one.

Khashair made no attempt to dodge.

When this one hit, the explosion rocked the village.

He flew back out of the protection of the spell circle.

Fane didn't hesitate.

She became one with the ether and appeared beside him, sword raised.

Instead of fear or horror, he wore a smile of pleasure.

Before her sword could fall, dark magic slammed into her.

Her body started to come apart the instant the spell touched her.

She tried to dissolve to no avail.

Resist as she might, the spell continued to rip her to pieces.

She didn't scream; Fane refused to give him the satisfaction. Besides, unlike a regular undead, she'd made arrangements should her physical form be destroyed.

Her contingency triggered just as she lost consciousness.

CHAPTER 33

The last of the fog was being drawn in to the mithril hoop. Joran hadn't been paying that close attention to the timing, but he guessed about half an hour had passed. Considering how much there was, that wasn't too bad. Even better, now they'd be able to explore the... village?

That didn't seem like quite the right word for the collection of buildings before them. Instead of houses, most of them were low, two- or three-story towers. The only truly big building was a black stone citadel in the center of the valley. Just looking at it gave him a shiver.

"How do you want to approach the search?" Alexandra asked.

"One tower at a time I suppose. I dislike the idea of separating. We'll collect any books or other valuables we find and bring them back here. Shouldn't take more than a few days to cover the whole area."

Mia shifted over beside him and whispered, "Someone's coming."

Joran closed his eyes and concentrated. A faint crunch like boots on gravel reached him. "You need to hide. You'll have a better chance of taking down whoever it is if they don't know you're coming."

She frowned, clearly not thrilled with the suggestion. Thankfully she slipped out of sight without an argument.

Joran turned to address the others. "Company coming. Let's get ready to greet them."

The others gathered around him, weapons drawn.

Half a minute later Samaritan strode into sight. He had a pair of black iron golems on either side of him and an especially arrogant sneer curling his lips. It was a different expression than anything Joran had seen before. He wore an odd device strapped to his arm. In the ether, the thing seethed with corrupt energy.

"I wanted to see who was responsible for helping me gain victory over the vampire. Imagine a raggedy group of humans and dwarves proving so useful." Samaritan or whoever was controlling his body cocked his head as if hearing something inaudible to the rest of them. "It seems we've met before. Joran Den Cade, I believe, along with Grub and Antius."

He focused on Alexandra. "You, however, are new to me. Last time we encountered each other, he had a different woman with him. I suppose he got bored with that one. Though bringing a woman to a place like this makes me think he isn't overly fond of you either."

Alexandra bristled but Joran hurried to cut off any outburst. "And who are you? I recognize Samaritan's body, but who's wearing it now?"

"You are a clever one. My name is Khashair and I was an overmage in the Black Iron Empire. Soon I will rule this land as well. Now that the only one powerful enough to stop me is dead, it's only a matter of time before I hunt down and elimi-nate the current rulers of this empire."

"Is that what you really want, Bellator?" Titus stepped between Joran and Alexandra. "You said we were going to create a new world, a better one. I hardly think an empire ruled by a former overmage qualifies."

Samaritan's face twisted. "No, not now!"

Power crackled around the device on his wrist and gathered around Samaritan's head.

Whatever was happening, it didn't look good.

Joran concentrated with all his will.

Now, Mia!

She sprinted in from the left, sword leading.

The golems tried to stop her, but the sword reduced them to scrap in a second.

That second proved costly.

Dark power shot out.

Mia cut it apart with her sword, but the force of the blast knocked her back two paces.

"There's our missing woman. And armed with a mithril sword. You, my dear, may be a greater threat than the vampire."

Mia stared, eyes narrow, looking for an opening.

"Bellator?" Titus asked.

"Don't waste your breath, boy. Your friend has been crushed down into the deepest recesses of my mind. He will not be rushing to rescue you this time."

"No!" Titus screamed and sprinted forward, fists raised like he planned to beat down Khashair with his bare hands.

Power gathered again around Khashair's hands.

Titus slammed into him from the front just as Mia ran him through the back.

His body went rigid and the ether smoothed.

The mithril sword made no distinction between friend and foe, piercing Titus through the chest.

Both men collapsed and a black mist rose out of Samaritan before shooting east out of sight.

Joran scrambled over beside his brother. "Titus! Let me see."

He rolled Titus over and grimaced. There was nothing to be

done. The sword had gone straight through his heart. Titus was dead before he hit the ground.

"Didn't want this for him," Samaritan gasped. "He was a good friend. Better than I deserved."

"Finally, something we can agree on," Joran said.

"It's not over. Khashair's soul has retreated to the artifact he left in my tower. There's a storeroom in the basement guarded by more golems. You have to destroy it or he'll eventually find a new host."

Joran cursed all wizards. "Where is this tower?"

"Not sure. East of here somewhere." Samaritan stared at the sky and let out his last breath. "We'll finally be together again."

And with that he died.

Mia knelt beside Joran. "I'm so sorry. I didn't mean to hit your brother too."

He took her hand. "I know you didn't. I think he wanted to die with his friend and save the family from the backlash that would come when everyone found out he'd been working with Samaritan."

There was a gentle touch on his back and Alexandra said, "Your brother died a hero and if anyone asks, that's what I'll tell them."

Joran sighed. That was even almost the truth. "Thank you."

"It's not over, you know."

They all scrambled up and spun toward the new voice. A boy, maybe twelve years old, walked into the clearing around the hoop. He wore a brown robe and carried a black iron sword.

"Beastmaster," Antius growled. His grip tightened so hard on his sword that Joran could hear the leather creak.

The youth brightened like he wasn't facing six-to-one odds. "I know you. Are these the people that got you out of my flesh pit? I bet the girl with the mithril sword killed my pets. Nothing else would cut through their fur so easily. I wish I could have seen how you did it so I could make improvements in the next batch."

He didn't seem interested in a fight which suited Joran very well. "Um, you said it wasn't over. Do you know where to find Khashair's artifact?"

"No, I was talking about Fane. Khashair destroyed her body, but her soul retreated to her restoration chamber. It's in the basement of the citadel." He pointed at the dark castle. "She'll regenerate in a week or so, assuming you don't go in there and finish her off."

"I'm assuming Fane is the name of the female vampire," Joran said. "I further assume that you two are allies. So why are you telling us that we need to kill her?"

"Allies might not be the right word," Beastmaster said. "Fane acts like I'm her employee and she treats me like it too. I'm sick of running her errands. It's exhausting. Taking over the world is a miserable project. I can't figure out why so many people keep trying to do it. I just want to conduct my experiments in peace. As long as she's alive, I can't do that."

"So you're not going to show up in Tiber and try to burn down the palace or something?" Alexandra asked.

Beastmaster cocked his head, making him look even younger. "Why would I do that? I create mutated beasts; I'm not a pyromaniac. You should hurry. Fane's defenses will only get stronger the longer she's in there."

Before Joran had a chance to ask any more questions, Beastmaster vanished.

"What an odd fellow," Mia said.

Odd or not, the information Beastmaster provided about the vampire was invaluable. "We'll leave Titus here for now. I want to finish quickly. Then we'll need to try and find this tower Samaritan mentioned."

"Are you okay to keep going?" Alexandra asked.

Joran let out another long sigh. "Doesn't matter. She's in there, getting stronger by the second. We need to move."

The group formed up and marched toward the castle. There was no gate on the side they approached from, so Joran led them around the perimeter until they found a raised drawbridge. There was no moat, so he wasn't sure what purpose it served beyond keeping people out. Though it certainly seemed effective at that.

"How do we get in?" Stoneheart asked.

Mia strode right up to the drawbridge, slashed three times, and kicked it. A rectangle of wood crashed inward, leaving a nearly perfect door. "How about that?"

"Works for me." Joran followed her in and looked around the courtyard. Nothing but dirt and emptiness.

There were a pair of outbuildings and Joran nodded toward the nearest. Stoneheart went for the door while Mia and Antius prepared to cut down whatever they found inside. When Stoneheart pulled, the hinges ripped out of the wood and he stumbled back. Inside they found only rusted metal and rotten wood.

The second, smaller building turned out to be totally empty. At least they wouldn't have to worry about something waiting to attack them when they left.

Mia led the way to the keep. A wooden door behind a black iron portcullis blocked access to the interior. They stood up to Mia's sword no better than the drawbridge had. Half a dozen slashes later and they were standing in a large entry hall done all in black stone.

"This place would be right at home in the Black Iron Empire," Grub muttered.

Joran couldn't deny that the aesthetic certainly matched despite being stone instead of metal. "We need to find a way to the basement. Everyone be on your guard and touch nothing until Grub or I tell you it's okay."

With that warning the group set out. A single hall led out of the entry area. Joran kept his vision on the ether. Corruption covered everything in a thick, black layer. It felt like the fog outside. Mia's sword dissolved most of it around them and Grub did something to keep the rest away. Joran didn't recognize the spell he used and didn't try to copy it. His skills remained too limited for something so complex.

Twenty strides into the fortress brought them to the first door. Magic sparked around the iron handle. No doubt it would do horrible things to whoever touched it.

"Grub, can you handle that?" Joran asked.

Grub frowned and said, "Move back."

Everyone retreated halfway down the hall.

When they were out of the way, an ethereal hand grasped the handle and pulled.

An explosion of dark energy burst out, filling the space they had just occupied.

Joran barely had time to process what happened when Mia sprinted up the hall.

Some kind of black dog with flames dripping from its jaws was headed right for her.

It opened its mouth like it was going to bark, and flames shot out.

Mia slid under them and swung.

The mithril sword sliced the beast in half and it vanished in a puff of stinking black smoke.

"Hell hound," Grub said in answer to his unasked question.

"Did that magic trap summon it?" Joran asked.

"No, that was a cloud of necromantic energy. The hell hound came from deeper in the fortress. Just be glad it wasn't a whole pack of them."

Joran was certainly glad of that. "Are you okay?"

Mia stood and nodded. A little wisp of smoke rose from her tunic, but her skin appeared unharmed.

They went to the now-safe-looking door. Antius pulled it

open without comment. Inside were wooden crates and chests stacked floor to ceiling.

Grub rubbed his hands together. "Treasure."

"Focus," Joran said. "We're looking for stairs down not loot."

They kept searching for what felt like hours. The process was the same at each door. Grub triggered the trap, Antius opened the door, and Mia killed anything supernatural that showed up. So far that included two more hell hounds, some strange undead that crawled along the ceiling, a flying lizard with a skull head and poisoned claws, and strangest of all a human head with tentacles growing out of its neck and eyes. That thing would haunt Joran's nightmares for the rest of his life.

Joran wiped sweat from his forehead and studied the descending staircase hidden in a small alcove behind the most recent door they'd opened. As far as he could tell, no magic protected it.

He glanced at Grub and the dwarf shook his head. "Looks clear to me."

"Would you mind scouting it out?" Joran asked. "I don't want to run blindly into an army of undead down there."

Grub closed his eyes and his ethereal construct flew out and down the stairs. "Bottom's clear. Not a light to be seen though. How far do you want me to go?"

"As far as you can."

"The hall's empty and lined with open, empty doors. I'll wager this is where the nasty things we ran into lived. I reached an intersection, going right. Three more empty chambers. Checking left."

Joran tapped his fingers on his biceps. Come on, he wanted this done.

"Uh-oh," Grub said. "I found the vampire, I think, but there's a problem. The final room is guarded by a dozen...things. I've never seen anything like them. Their skin is gray and smooth.

They've got claws and fangs to spare and the blackest eyes I've ever seen."

"Some kind of bile monsters, I'm sure." Joran opened his kit and pulled out six adhesive vials. They were so handy he'd taken to carrying more than usual. "Do you think magic will work on them?"

"Only one way to find out," Grub said.

"Figured you'd say that."

Mia held up her sword. "This will work on them."

"I'm sure, but twelve against one is a lot even for you. I'm hoping we can bind a few of them before we attack. Even the odds a bit."

Joran handed three vials to Grub and kept the rest for himself. "Smash them at their feet. If you can get more than one, so much the better."

Extending his sight and carrying a single vial took everything Joran had. When he saw the monsters for himself, he shuddered. Grub's description didn't do them justice. They were even more horrifying than the tentacle-head thing.

The nearest one stared at the floating vial but made no move to attack. It probably didn't consider the vial a threat. Joran would disabuse it of that idea quickly.

An effort of will shattered the vial directly above the nearest creature's feet. The adhesive oozed out and quickly hardened locking the monster in place. While Joran sent a second vial floating down, Grub stuck down five with his vials. Someone took his final vial out of his hand.

He didn't argue. Grub was clearly better at this than him.

At least he managed to hit his second target.

In the end they ended up sticking eight of the things to the floor, leaving four still mobile. Far from ideal, but better than twelve.

Joran returned his sight to his body and gasped. That took

way more out of him than he'd expected. "We did all we could. Mia, Antius, Stoneheart, you're up."

The warriors strode toward the stairs with Mia in the lead. Joran moved to follow but Alexandra caught his hand. "They can handle it. You need to rest."

He didn't even try to argue. Instead, he moved to the top of the steps beside Grub and listened. The thuds and slices of combat reached them soon enough.

"You did good," Grub said. "Didn't figure you had enough focus for two spells at the same time. Glad I was wrong."

"I'm not anxious to try it again. How is it you're not exhausted?"

Grub shrugged. "Fifty years more experience than you."

"I suppose that would make a difference."

Everything went quiet then Mia said, "We're good."

Right, back to work.

Joran led the others downstairs and grimaced at the mess filling the hall. Bits of monsters and puddles of black blood covered the floor. None of the warriors had been hurt which came as a relief. The door at the end of the hall crackled with the most powerful trap Joran had seen yet.

"I'll handle it," Grub said.

They all moved well back and the dwarf used the same magic construct as before to grasp the handle.

This time fire and lightning exploded from all directions. When the fury subsided, only piles of ash filled the hall. Nice of her to leave a clean-up mechanism behind.

"It's clear," Grub said.

Inside the final room waited a crystal coffin charged with more ethereal energy than Joran had ever seen. Inside the coffin floated a vaguely female-shaped cloud of dark energy. Joran could only think of one way to do this.

"Mia, you're up. Thrust your sword into that dark cloud and let the mithril purify it."

She gave the crystal the side-eye. "You think it'll cut through crystal?"

"It cuts through everything else. Only one way to find out for sure."

Mia leapt up on the coffin and slammed the tip of her sword into it. As Joran expected, the mithril sliced right through. The only thing that had given them trouble was that Hell-forged sword the assassin used. Everything else might as well be paper.

The sword seemed to draw the darkness into it. Second by second the dark cloud grew smaller until at last the coffin was empty.

Somehow Joran had expected something else to happen. That he'd get some kind of sign that it was really over.

Mia took his hand and hopped down. "Did I do it?"

"As far as I can tell. Now we need to find Khashair's hideout."

"Now you need to rest," Alexandra said in her Iron Princess voice.

That sounded good too. "Grub, can you do something to secure the fortress? I don't want someone finding and looting this place before we get back."

"I can ward the entrance," Grub said. "It won't stop a really powerful wizard, like that kid, but it'll stop some random thief that might wander into the valley."

"Good enough."

Now that the immediate danger had passed, all he wanted to do was sleep. Grief and exhaustion combined to nearly over-whelm him.

Somehow Joran held it together until they made it back to the dragon ship. When he and Alexandra were alone, he cried himself to sleep in her arms.

CHAPTER 34

Joran didn't know how long he slept, but when he finally woke, he felt better than he expected. Knowing Titus's magically preserved body was lying in the hold of the dragon ship draped with a tarp put a little catch in his throat, but it was nothing he couldn't force his way through. At least as long as he didn't think about the conversation he was going to have to have with his family when he got home.

He rolled out of his hammock and looked around at the empty cabin. Alexandra must be on the bridge. A moment of concentration confirmed that Mia was with her. He had no idea about the others, but felt certain they'd be ready when the time came.

Assuming they found the tower Samaritan mentioned.

Joran dressed and made his way up to the bridge. It felt empty without the Iron Guards. But given what they were doing, the fewer people who knew about it the better.

As soon as he stepped through the door Mia hurried over. "Are you okay?"

He offered a weak smile. "As okay as possible considering. Did you get a little rest?"

"Yeah, I'm good, though it felt weird having the cabin to myself. I knew you were right next door, but it wasn't the same."

His gaze shifted to Alexandra, who kept a few paces away. "Any luck?"

She shook her head. "Nothing yet. We may end up needing the other dragon ship to expand the search."

That didn't especially surprise him. There was a lot of territory out here, all of it wild. Finding a single tower, especially if it was damaged and not jutting above the trees, was a big job. It still needed to be done. Having the overmage's soul sitting out there like a delayed-action alchemy bomb wasn't something the empire could allow.

"Has Grub been up here?" Joran asked.

"No, why?" Alexandra asked.

"Well, if this is a wizard's tower, we might be able to see something in the ether. Some magical spark to guide us."

"Want me to go get him?" Mia asked.

"Not right now. I can look until my eyes get tired then he can take over."

Joran walked up to the window and shifted his vision to the ether. The instant he did, he found the usually chaotic energy field looked especially orderly a few miles further north. It was worth checking out.

"Turn north and just a little more east. I don't know what it is, but something's there."

Joran caught the captain's faint sigh before he relayed the order. Soon enough the dragon ship changed course and they were headed right toward the anomaly.

A twenty-minute flight brought them within sight of a broken stone tower. The top looked like a catapult stone had hit it full on. Rubble littered the modest clearing. Since it hadn't been transformed to black iron, Joran figured the dragon didn't smash it, though he couldn't imagine what had.

Well, as long as whatever it was didn't decide to come back in the next hour or so, he didn't really care.

"Is that it?" Alexandra asked.

"Seems like it has to be, but there's only one way to be sure."

"Right, let's go." Alexandra turned to leave, but Joran put a gentle hand on her arm. "What?"

"Would you mind staying up here?" When she started to object, he raised his hands. "I know you want to help and I'm grateful, but if there are black iron golems down there, your sword won't even scratch them. I'm leaving Antius behind for the same reason."

Even scowling she was beautiful. "Fine, but if you get yourself killed, I swear I'll find a way to resurrect you and kill you myself."

Joran kissed her. "Thanks."

On the way to the gondola, Joran and Mia picked up the dwarves. As they walked, Joran described what he saw in the ether.

"Sounds like a barrier," Grub said. "Probably to stop anyone from scrying on him. Shouldn't be a problem since we're here in the flesh."

Joran had about had his fill of shoulds, but doubted he'd get anything better. In the hold they loaded into the gondola and began the descent.

———

Mia clenched and relaxed her right hand as the gondola descended. Joran's pain at his brother's death had nearly broken her heart. The fact that she killed Titus made the ache even more visceral. She really hadn't meant to do it and she knew Joran didn't blame her. Their link revealed his true feelings and there was nothing but love for her there.

It was an extremely generous reaction.

"You alright?" Joran shifted to stand closer to her.

She forced her hand to go still. "Yeah, just ready for this to be over."

"You said it. Though I think I'd rather face another giant serpent than tell my parents about Titus."

"I'm sorr—"

"Stop apologizing. I know you didn't mean to do it. And frankly, telling them how he died will be easier than telling them how he betrayed their trust."

She stared for a moment. "You're going to tell them everything?"

He nodded. "They deserve to know the whole truth. How much we tell Camellia and the boys is another matter altogether. That will be up to Mother and Father. My guess is that they'll keep most of it to themselves."

The gondola hit the ground and Mia hurried to get out ahead of Joran. Whatever happened, she refused to let him get hurt again.

Many booted feet had trod down the grass and dirt near the entrance. The clearing was absolutely silent. They were in the middle of the forest. Where were the birds and squirrels? Everything about the situation felt wrong.

"Samaritan said the artifact was in the basement," Joran said. "Let's see if we can find the entrance."

Mia made sure to lead the way inside. Not that there was anything particularly threatening. A set of rickety steps led to the second floor. There was nothing that indicated the tower even had a basement.

"Grub?" Joran said.

The dwarf wizard did something, Mia couldn't see it, but she sensed it through her link with Joran. A few seconds later a trapdoor appeared out of nowhere.

"He hid it with an illusion," Grub said. "If you didn't know to look, I never would have guessed it was there."

"I saw nothing in the ether," Joran said.

"Of course not. The illusion is useless if you can see through it with your magical sight."

Mia ignored the magical discussion and focused on the trapdoor. And lucky she did. It slammed open and the head of a black iron golem poked out.

She dropped and slashed, cutting its head off and sending it tumbling back down the stone stairs.

"Well done." Joran gave her a pat on the back. "Let's see what else is down there."

Mia closed her eyes and focused on their link. If she concentrated really hard, sometimes she caught a glimpse of what Joran did. A short tunnel led to a large chamber filled with racks that held black swords and armor. There was also a cabinet with a vial-filled rack on top. Beside the rack sat a black iron sphere. Though no wizard, Mia knew that had to be the artifact.

The image vanished and Joran turned toward her. His face was scrunched up in the expression he got when he was thinking hard.

"What is it?"

"Assuming that's the artifact and further assuming Khashair's soul is inside of it, he'll likely try to kill anyone that gets close. Remember what Alexandra told us—according to the church, the artifact killed anyone that touched it. He might be able to attack from a distance as well."

"Okay, so what do we do?"

Joran chewed his lip. She could rarely remember him being this hesitant.

"You need to go in alone and destroy the orb. Khashair uses corrupt ether, and the mithril will protect you. If any of the rest of us get close..."

"I understand. If this is something I can do, then I'll do it."

"I know it's impossible for you to be careful, but please try."

Mia grinned. "You're not getting rid of me that easily."

Her quip did nothing to lessen his anxiety. Mia didn't really think it would, but she had to try.

A deep breath steadied her and she descended the stairs. A ball of white light appeared beside her revealing a tunnel that led to a cavern the size of a small warehouse. Everything looked exactly as she saw it through Joran's spell only clearer. The black orb, despite its small size, seemed to dominate the room.

She raised her sword, putting it between her and the orb. When nothing happened, she marched forward, determined to destroy the evil thing and get out of here.

Do you truly wish to destroy me?

She frowned and paused in her advance. Was Khashair going to try and bribe her now? If he could project his voice into her mind, surely he could read enough of her thoughts to know there was no way she'd be swayed.

That's your soulmate talking. He has power, wealth, and is soon to marry into the imperial family. All you have are the scraps he tosses you. Join me and together we could rule the empire.

She nearly laughed. Did he imagine she'd betray the only person that had ever loved her while wanting nothing in return?

Mia resumed her advance. The world would be a better place without this monster in it.

She raised her sword and brought it down hard.

A hemisphere of dark energy tried to stop her blade.

And it succeeded, for about two seconds.

Like everything else it encountered, the mithril sword cut through the spell and continued on through the orb and the cabinet beneath it.

She winced. Hopefully there was nothing in there Joran wanted.

A black cloud rose out of the destroyed orb and she got ready for another fight.

There wasn't one.

The cloud dissipated and soon she was alone in the chamber.

Seconds passed and nothing else attacked her. Satisfied that she'd completed her mission, Mia sheathed her sword and hurried back upstairs.

As soon as she reached the top, Joran hugged her. "I never doubted you could do it."

"I know you didn't. Your confidence gives me strength. How about we get out of here? I want to go home."

"Excellent idea, though we'll have to pick up the emperor and the pope, along with their entourages, on our way."

She didn't care what they had to do, as long as they ended up in Tiber. Mia had had enough fighting for a long time.

EPILOGUE

S pring in the gardens of the imperial palace was
stunning. Pink blossoms covered scores of cherry trees
and every time the wind blew it sent hundreds of them
swirling around. The wedding, Joran and Alexandra's—every
time he thought that it felt unreal—was set to happen at noon.

Joran stood on a little hill beside Mia. He wore formal
crimson and gold robes and she had on a crisp new Iron Guard
uniform. As always, the mithril sword was belted at her waist.
When they picked the pope up at the Fourth Legion's barracks,
he hadn't even tried to demand its return. Joran very much
appreciated that since it saved him the trouble of saying no
again. The weapon was far too useful to sit unused in the
church's basement.

And speaking of the pope, Septimus himself stood to Joran's
right. He wore his formal robes of office, including a third
stupid hat. This one looked a bit like a church steeple and had
The One God's circle drawn on the front. Though Joran
doubted his sincerity, Septimus did a credible job of looking
pleased to be officiating over the wedding.

A crowd of nobles thronged the garden. Joran had gotten a

reprieve from mingling, at least until after the ceremony. His parents and even Quintus, looking remarkably sober, were watching from the front of the crowd. When Joran told them about Titus, they'd been shocked, horrified, and saddened by his death. Once that passed, Father went straight to furious. He couldn't believe Titus would betray them to Den March Trading, old friendship be damned. Mother had just cried softly without saying a word.

That had been nearly two months ago. They held Titus's funeral a week after Joran got home and spread his ashes in the garden. Betrayer or not, he was still a Den Cade and received all the honor that entailed.

Father had gotten over the shock more quickly than Mother, but even she seemed okay despite the constant air of sadness that clung to her. It helped that Quintus had turned over a new leaf and was even helping with the business.

According to Father, that was a miracle on par with anything he'd ever experienced. Joran thought he was exaggerating, but it was still a surprise and a pleasant one for a change.

Somewhere out of sight, a minstrel struck a chord and everyone fell silent. The emperor entered the garden with Alexandra holding his arm.

Joran's breath caught in his throat. She wore a crimson wedding dress that clung to her in a very fetching way. Her hair was accented with gold beads. She wore no other jewelry and needed none. She was the most beautiful woman in the garden if not the empire. From the excitement flooding their link, Mia agreed.

The emperor wore crimson and gold formal robes and the eagle crown on his brow.

They stopped beside Joran and Alexandra transferred her grasp to his arm while the emperor moved a few paces way.

"You look stunning."

She smiled. "Thank you. I had my doubts that we'd make it to this day."

"I'm glad we did." He didn't add that thinking about this moment helped him fight through the many deadly obstacles they'd faced.

Septimus cleared his throat and everyone fell silent. "We are gathered here today under the watchful gaze of The One God to join Joran Den Cade and Alexandra Tiberius in the bonds of marriage."

He turned to Joran. "Do you take this woman as your wife, to be together in good times and bad until The One God calls you home?"

"I do," Joran said without a moment's hesitation.

Septimus turned to Alexandra. "Do you take this man as your husband, to be together in good times and bad until The One God calls you home?"

"I do," Alexandra said with equal eagerness.

"Then I declare you wed. You may kiss the bride."

That was one holy directive Joran was happy to obey.

When they came up for air Septimus continued. "May the happy couple live a long and prosperous life in our glorious empire. So say we all."

"So say we all!" the crowd thundered.

Joran pulled Alexandra close and whispered in her ear. "So say we all."

AUTHOR NOTE

Hello everyone,

I hope you've enjoyed The Soul Bound Saga. I certainly had a lot of fun writing it. If you'd like to keep up with my writing, you can join my weekly newsletter, you'll find the sign up form on the homepage of my website.

You can also join me for my regular Sunday livestream on my YouTube channel here. https://www.youtube.com/@ JamesEWisherbooks

You can find links to all my books on my website, www. jamesewisher.com

Thanks for reading and I'll see you next time.

James

ALSO BY JAMES E WISHER

The Soul Bound Saga

An Unwelcome Journey

Darkness in Tiber

Depths of Betrayal

The Black Iron Empire

Overmage

The Divine Key Trilogy

Shadow Magic

For The Greater Good

The Divine Key Awakens

The Portal Wars Saga

The Hidden Tower

The Great Northern War

The Portal Thieves

The Master of Magic

The Chamber of Eternity

The Heart of Alchemy

The Sanguine Scroll

The Dragonspire Chronicles

The Black Egg

The Mysterious Coin

The Dragons' Graveyard

The Slave War

The Sunken Tower

The Dragon Empress

The Dragonspire Chronicles Omnibus Vol. 1

The Dragonspire Chronicles Omnibus Vol. 2

The Complete Dragonspire Chronicles Omnibus

Soul Force Saga

Disciples of the Horned One Trilogy:

Darkness Rising

Raging Sea and Trembling Earth

Harvest of Souls

Disciples of the Horned One Omnibus

Chains of the Fallen Arc:

Dreaming in the Dark

On Blackened Wings

Chains of the Fallen Omnibus

The Complete Soul Force Saga Omnibus

The Aegis of Merlin:

The Impossible Wizard

The Awakening

The Chimera Jar

The Raven's Shadow

Escape From the Dragon Czar

Wrath of the Dragon Czar

The Four Nations Tournament

Death Incarnate

Atlantis Rising

Rise of the Demon Lords

The Pale Princess

Aegis of Merlin Omnibus Vol 1.

Aegis of Merlin Omnibus Vol 2.

The Complete Aegis of Merlin Omnibus

Other Fantasy Novels:

The Squire

Death and Honor Omnibus

The Rogue Star Series:

Children of Darkness

Children of the Void

Children of Junk

Rogue Star Omnibus Vol. 1

Children of the Black Ship

ABOUT THE AUTHOR

James E. Wisher is a writer of science fiction and fantasy novels. He's been writing since high school and reading everything he could get his hands on for as long as he can remember.

To learn more:
www.jamesewisher.com
james@jamesewisher.com

Ingram Content Group UK Ltd.
Milton Keynes UK
UKHW011531040723
424531UK00001B/67